A Drey in the Life of Tipple Squirrel

by

Bruce MacDonald

Foreword

Hello! Nice tae meet ye! My name's Tipple Squirrel and I'm a Scottish MacRed with a family consisting of my wife Suzy Squirrel and three bairns or kits as we call them. Being a squirrel these days is not so easy as you would think and as well as making a living and gathering food, we have to avoid environmental dangers and meat-eating animals and birds. Then there are the dreaded humans! In an effort to make the life of a squirrel better known to you humans, I have recounted my most recent adventures to my friend Bruce MacDonald. As a result, there's now no excuse for not knowing about a red squirrel's life and what we need to stay happy and healthy. I'm sure there's enough room in Scotland for animals and people to live together - we squirrels don't take up a lot of space. We just need a peaceful, healthy forest and a plentiful supply of nuts. Below is a list of addresses on what you humans call the Internet to find out more about red squirrel populations. Well, a hae tae gang now, but I'll be back again sometime. Guid cheerio the nou!

Tipple MacRed Squirrel of that Ilk.

www.saveoursquirrels.org.uk
www.scottishsquirrels.org.uk
www.rsst.org.uk
www.snh.gov.uk/docs/A409170.pdf
www.red-squirrels.org.uk
www.europeansquirrelinitiative.org

CHAPTERS

Foreword

Part One

Part Two

Part Three

Part One

The MacRed Family

It was winter in Hawick and a deep blanket of snow lay over the hardened ground in nearby Craik Forest. The trees were bare and silhouetted against a grey, foreboding sky and a sharp frost had anything unmovable in its grip. It is hard at this time of year for most animals - and Tipple MacRed Squirrel was no exception. For a squirrel of his size, the blanket of snow was like a pile of duvets. His memory was not what it used to be, and on this day he was having difficulty locating his cache of nuts from the autumn. Not only had he forgotten where they were. The ground was so frozen that he could hardly dig into the upper soil and this involved a veritable construction site to remove the snow.

Fortunately, he had not buried them so deep, and after frantically scraping the ground with his feet and front paws and a piece of stone he had found, he was able to locate a stash of six hazelnuts. What a feeling of elation after all the hard work!

Suddenly, Tipple was uneasy and stood erect to check his vicinity. He had also caught the odour of an animal that was not a squirrel. For some moments there was a deathly silence and nothing moved, but the odour remained and Tipple was on high alert. He saw nothing though and half relaxed. This was a grave mistake. No sooner had he turned his attention once more to the nuts, there was a sudden flourish and the snow began to move in his direction! He didn't wait to see what it was. He knew he was in danger and instinctively turned and dashed to the nearest tree, but as he climbed up the trunk he knew that he was being pursued. He zigzagged his way upwards with the odour of musk and the sound of squealing close behind him. Once he had gained sufficient height he moved across a branch but still the pursuer was behind him. His last chance was to jump to another tree which he did and then to another and another. The chasing animal was outwitted and remained motionless and frustrated.

Tipple regained his breath and stared back at the source of danger which was now descending the first tree. It was an ermine or stoat in its winter coat and thoroughly camouflaged against the snow on the ground. He waited until the animal disappeared into the snowy waste once more and then waited and waited until there was no sound or odour. The ermine had not seen his nuts and Tipple was not going to leave them for any old scavenger! He jumped to

"Is that a squirrel?"

the second tree and then the first and slowly descended to the snow once more. Looking and listening and sniffing the air, Tipple then made a dash for the nuts and stuffed them into his mouth with his front paws, before scampering back up the tree to safe heights. Jumping artistically from branch to branch, he made his way deeper into the wood where he located his drey at the top of a stately beech tree. Home at last and ready for a family meal although fully out of breath!

Tipple Squirrel

Let me introduce you to the family. Tipple the father, Suzy the mother, and three bairns or kits - Tim, Jenny and Angus in order of birth. Tipple is a handsome specimen with copper-looking red fur, tufted ears, a long, bushy tail and large, vigilant eyes. He is also an athlete in a fur coat and whilst his memory is not what it was, he is a practical type, inquisitive and industrious. Suzy is equally good-looking but somewhat smaller than Tipple and a stickler for tidiness. She also has a pure white undercoat that Tipple used to envy. Tim is the eldest of the kits, with Jenny the second in line, and then there is Angus, the real bairn of the family. The drey is quite a large one with a small opening just big enough for squirrels and just small enough to keep out large intruders. The floor is covered with leaves and moss and pine needles, except for one area which is used as a larder and dining area. Slightly higher up is another narrow opening which lets in the light and which also acts as an escape route.

How they all squealed with delight as Tipple returned from his food foray! There was only one problem - five family members and six nuts! Who was going to get the sixth? Tipple decided to store the sixth hazelnut in the larder area which was out of bounds to the kits except at meal times. After first drying the nuts in moss, it was time to tuck in.
"Delicious - a vintage year!" exclaimed Tipple to the rest of the family. They hungrily agreed, making quick work of the nuts, but Tipple was a connoisseur and slowly savoured every minute of his meal.

After dining, all the family retired to the rear of the drey, which had been made into a large sleeping area. There they snoozed away the afternoon until Tipple felt from his inner clock that it was time for another foray before sundown. First they were preoccupied with grooming themselves and then each other for ticks or fleas, and this procedure lasted several minutes. Soon they were ready and the whole family set out to visit their local friend Benjamin Badger. They sprang acrobatically from branch to branch and tree to tree, until after some ten to fifteen minutes they reached the locality where Badger lived. Now it was time to descend from the treetops, and head-first, they all scrambled down the somewhat snowy and mossy trunk.

Benjamin Badger lived in a sort of burrow which he called a sett. They never knew why it was called so. They presumed it was due to the fact that he was peculiarly set in his ways, or so they all thought. Tipple was the first to arrive at the entrance and clutching a large acorn, he threw this into the burrow.
"Ouch!" exclaimed a somewhat consternated creature from within.
"Oh, it's you Tipple."

They were soon joined by the other members of the squirrel family. The children especially loved to listen to Badger's stories from long ago and he was a great storyteller. It was a welcome change for Tim, Jenny and Angus from their school assignments, and very soon all were glued to Benjamin's account of a time long ago when all the animals lived together in peace and security.

"There was no danger then from foxes or wildcats, or from eagles pouncing on you from above. Even humans were friendly and could be trusted. All sorts of delicious food was available and no animal would starve in the winter. You could fill up your tummy and your larder to your heart's content," said Badger. "Nobody was afraid of going out during the day and all the animals were able to communicate with each other much better than they do today. No-one wanted to eat anyone else, and all the animals together with the birds were able to feed on the rich supply of nuts, berries, fruits, grass and vegetables left over in the fields by the humans. There were cultivated fields of course, but these were interspersed with hedges, bushes and woodland and roads were few and far between.

Indeed, there were forests so vast," continued Badger, "that some animals say they even caught sight of a unicorn!

There were very few large towns and most of the humans lived in villages spread over all the hospitable land. They used horses and donkeys to move about quickly and there was no roadkill from cars or loud noises from aeroplanes like today. Spring, summer and autumn were pleasant affairs with warm, balmy days and light breezes and although the high summer could be sultry and the winters came with snow, there were no deep frosts to freeze your paws in those days.

Most humans could be trusted in fact, and they used to let us feed from their hands. The children of the humans were also friendly, not so boisterous and mischievous like today. In fact, the farmers even let us enter their barns and storehouses in the winters for food and refuge as long as we didn't take too much and didn't stay too long! Everyone knew his neighbours and there was a bond of friendship between the animals that stayed put for generations.

The best thing of all," said Badger, "was that there was no school! All our children were brought up at home by their parents and taught how to climb, dig, fly, swim, run and to find food and water."
"Yippee!" exclaimed the young ones and then pertinently asked why that can't be so today.
Badger replied, "The times have changed, I'm afraid. It's not so easy to find food these days and you have to be taught how to hunt, how not to be caught, how to camouflage yourself, how to build a home and how to navigate your way around. Then there are the humans who are our biggest threat. How would you deal with them if you were chased by one of their dogs?"

The children thought about their school at Oak Hollow. This was presided over by Owl who was an expert on survival and full of practical wisdom and tips at the same time. All the animals attended the school and were given lessons until lunchtime after which they could put into practice all that they had learned. School in fact was an ongoing process until maturity as an adult as there was always something new to learn from wise old Owl. He had in fact been running Oak Hollow for many years and no-one really knew how long that was or how old he really was. All the animals, including the three squirrel children, tried to guess his age but it was no use. Owl was too wise to reveal this closely guarded secret.

Suddenly, the friends were disturbed by a loud barking. It was a dog at the entrance to the den! Everyone kept motionless and Badger pointed to a rear entrance, but Tipple was intent on misleading the hound. He rushed to the rear entrance, made sure that everything was clear and then scuttled out to see a large St. Bernhard dog still barking at the entrance. Tipple made himself apparent and zigzagged his way to a nearby tree in an effort to confuse the hound. The dog pursued him but was unable to climb up the trunk of the conifer tree where Tipple paused some feet above, his body pressed close to the trunk and his face appearing from behind. Tipple threw down twigs and branches but the dog continued his efforts to reach the squirrel.

"Come here, Bernie!" exclaimed a human, and the dog reluctantly left its prey to return to its master. Tipple observed that it was only a young couple out for a walk and not a hunter and his dog and he scampered down the tree back to Badger and his den. They were all mighty relieved to see Tipple and were happy that the dog had gone.

"That was a close shave," said Badger as he embraced Tipple for his bravery. "It's good that you can climb trees. I wish that I could. You know the humans breed dogs that look like sausages that can even squeeze into my sett."

After all the excitement, it was time to return to the drey before darkness fell. They were all looking forward to the last hazelnut in the larder and after some conversation and a lot of questions from the children, they retired to bed. Tomorrow was a day at school for the kits and a day of hunting for Tipple. He was intent on finding the nuts that he had buried in the autumn and he had difficulty in falling off to sleep for pure consternation!

A map of Craik Forest

A Bleak Winter

©Courtesy of Tomi Tapio, Wikimedia Commons. "What are we to eat?"

Tipple's hunting the next day was not going very well. He usually relied on his sense of smell as he had rubbed every nut with affection on his face only a few months ago before burying them so that he would know which were his. The problem was that thick snow was covering the ground and it was snowing heavily again.

Tipple knew that the nuts were about 100 yards from the drey in the direction of the sunset but he was having difficulty seeing now too, so heavy were the snowflakes that fell before his eyes and on his red fur. A jay was on the forest floor busily scrambling around in the snow and Tipple realized that his nut store may be right there. The jays were always trying to observe and outdo him and then make off with some of his cache. He scrambled down the trunk of an old oak tree and almost disappeared in the snow as he jumped on to the ground. The jay took a fright and scolding loudly, flew off into the bushes.

Tipple started to dig with paws and face here, there and everywhere but to no avail. The nuts were not to be found, and after half an hour or so, his paws were so frozen he was rapidly losing body temperature. He decided to jump back up the oak again to get a better view of the terrain but he could see nothing in the blizzard and the dim light below. There was nothing else for it - they would have to make do with tree bark today, and he pulled some of the bark off the top of the oak tree with his still cold front paws.

As he was heading back to the drey, he saw some deer down below also looking for food. They too were having problems, and just before reaching home he met some hares who had not eaten anything for three whole days. "We must do something quickly," thought Tipple and he made up his mind there and then to visit Badger again.

The next day, bright and early, the children left for school and Tipple and Suzy made their way through the thick snow to Badger's den.
"There is nothing else for it!" exclaimed an equally hungry Badger, "We will have to visit a farm."

The next day after he had managed to contact many other animals, a meeting was held in a secluded clearing not too far from Badger's den. The animals were all unanimous - something had to be done to solve the food problem - and a raid on one of the many farms in the area was the only reasonable solution to their plight. It was time to draw up a plan.
"Where can we get at the stored food most easily?" asked one of the hares. Owl and Badger drew up a plan of action, and Owl and two black ravens agreed to be the look-outs at the farm itself. They didn't want to take any of the food from the farm animals, although this was supplied regularly every day, and so the first target was to be the organic waste bin, followed by the grain silo and then the chicken run. It was decided that the party, consisting of Tipple Squirrel, Badger, three weasels, four hares and Angus the Stag, would carry out their raid in the early hours of the next morning, sometime after midnight. All the food collected would be shared out equally amongst the animals at the clearing but, of course, according to taste.

Meeting once again at the clearing in their thickest winter coats, and just after twelve chimes had been rung in nearby Hawick, the animals set out led by Badger and Tipple. The moon was shining brightly on the fields as the animals coldly pressed on against a chill wind, guided by Owl and the two ravens above. It was not long before they were in sight of a farmhouse and they kept close together as they approached, making sure that everyone and everything, including the Border Collie, were fast asleep. The house and the stalls were in darkness, and they made themselves ready for the ambush.

Tipple and the weasels approached the refuse bins near the big barn opposite the house to carry out phase one of the plan. Badger had provided them with a piece of rope he had collected some time in the past, and Tipple tied it to the handle of the green bin's lid. Then, carefully retiring, Badger and Angus pulled on the rope. Off went the lid, the thick snow damping any commotion, and Tipple and the weasels returned to inspect the contents. There were a lot of vegetable peelings, which didn't really appeal to any of them, but also pieces of half-eaten cake with walnuts! Tipple pulled off the nuts whilst the weasels found the remains of several loaves of bread still in good condition. Digging deeper, there was bread with cheese and honey and some remains of a chocolate bar, also with nuts! They passed everything down to the hares, who filled a sack that Badger and Angus were holding open with excitement and anticipation.
"Great work," exclaimed Badger, "but we must press on to phase two."

Phase two involved getting in to the grain silo but that wasn't really necessary as there was a substantial amount of barley on the floor in front of it. Badger took hold of a wooden shovel and filled the grain into another sack they had found, held open by the antlers of Angus. After only a few moments, it was full and Badger secured it on the back of Angus with the other sack from the organic snatch. From there they moved on to the manure heap.

Phase three, as they called it, again involved Tipple and the weasels. They scurried down to the compost and manure heap where they waited for Badger. Despite the freezing temperature, some of the material was fresh and soft, but Badger also lit some candles he had collected and placed them underneath the snow-covered edges to help things along. Soon everything was ready and Tipple and the weasels put on their camouflage. They covered their heads and shoulders with the now soft compost and manure and then applied a coating of straw. In the moonlight they looked like small, pink scarecrows. They then scurried off again in the direction of the henhouse. Once there, they saw that the opening to the house was large enough for all of them to creep silently into the eerie interior. Squeaking and wailing suddenly at the top of their voices, the four creatures lit up the candles, also provided by the ever-resourceful Badger. All that the poor, slumbering hens saw were hideous faces together with a terrible noise, and for such a fright they laid several eggs, and then flew in panic around the henhouse. Tipple and the weasels quickly gathered up the warm eggs and made a daring escape the same way that they had come to the other waiting animals who hardly recognized them as they were now covered in more straw and feathers.

The commotion had stirred up the Border Collie from his slumbers and there was a loud barking. It wasn't long before a light came on in the farmhouse and the dog rushed out of the unlocked door to see what was going on. Confused by all the different scents from the various animal friends, it went this way and that way without seeing the group. The friends made a quick exit from the farm, were soon lost in the nearby woods and in safety, at least for the time being. The farmer and his wife looked in consternation at the overturned waste bin and the hundreds of different paw marks all over the snow. Across at the henhouse, things had settled down but the farmer's wife thought that they had been visited by a fox and went to count the hens. Everything was in one piece but what had been going on?!

The animal friends made their way back to the clearing feeling much warmer after all the excitement, and there they counted out and shared the spoil, Badger once again providing several straw bags to make the carrying easier. Tipple was the only one really interested in the walnuts but he also took two of the eggs. There was in fact enough for everyone for at least a week, and once they had bidden a warm farewell to one another, they left for their respective homes and their much-postponed sleep.

Tipple arrived back at the drey and woke up a bleary-eyed Suzy.
"Look what we have to eat," said a still excited Tipple, and he opened up two of the bags. There was some bread with seeds, walnuts and two whole eggs. What a feast! Poached eggs for breakfast in every sense of the word! But now it was time to retire. The next day was to be a dream come true for Tipple.

Hidden Treasure

Some days later, when things had settled down to normal again, or as normal as it could be in mid-winter, Tipple and Suzy were out foraging in the forest. They confidently skipped from tree to tree and then made their way down to lower ground. It was a Sunday, and a time to be on guard, as many humans were out walking through the woods with their dogs. Actually Tipple was quite used to this and often led the pooches a merry dance as he jumped on to the ground, made himself visible to the dog, and then scurried up the nearest tree to a safe height, leaving the poor thing barking helplessly at the foot of the trunk! Still, it was always wise to be cautious.

It was mid-afternoon and still light enough for many walkers to be out for recreational purposes. Tipple and Suzy Squirrel thus stayed half-way up the tree trunks. In the high branches they fraternised with thrushes, blackbirds, and the occasional robin and learnt that food was scarce once again in the whole district. Climbing down a little, they caught sight of William Hedgehog on the forest floor. He was particularly bright and breezy this afternoon and the squirrels noticed that he was clutching something in his paws. As they drew nearer, Tipple discovered, much to his delight, that William was holding two acorns.
"Hello William! What do you have there?" asked a curious Tipple.
"Nothing in particular," replied William rather reluctantly, "I just found these two buried in a patch over yonder."
"Over yonder?" exclaimed an excited Tipple. "Where exactly?"
As he approached William more closely, he sniffed at the acorns.
"Why, those are mine!" he said, "Though I don't mind you keeping those two. But where exactly did you find them?"
"Come with me and I'll show you the exact location."

William had a very good memory, unlike Tipple of late, and although he was slow and pedantic, Tipple and Suzy followed closely behind keeping a sharp lookout for predators. William pointed to a hole that he had dug through the snow and into the earth.
"This is it! My cache of acorns!" exclaimed a highly excited Tipple.
"You're a marvel, William Hedgehog!" and Tipple picked him up by the front paws and they danced a little jig. Tipple looked nervously around for any pesky Jays but there were none, and so he told Suzy to return home and

fetch bags and the three children as quickly as possible. He then started to dig an area of one metre in circumference here, there and everywhere.

Yes, it was his nut cache alright and he had soon dug out a dozen or so. Shortly after, Suzy and the bairns returned with the bags and were soon involved in filling them to the brim. Tipple was very industrious as he wanted to get all his nuts out of the earth as soon as possible and stored in the drey's larder. It was also getting dusky though and this added to his ferocious activity. Soon, he felt that he had all his hidden treasure, and in total they had 7 or 8 bags full. Tipple gave one of these to his friend William and then they scurried up the pine trees and over the treetops clutching and holding in their mouths the many bags.

As they arrived home, the acorns were quickly emptied into the larder - all but five for the evening's supper! Once they had washed and dried the acorns, all sat down for the feast. It was a very romantic atmosphere with the cold snow outside, the acorns from last year and the warm, cosy drey. Everyone was very happy and after the meal, the children were able to play around the opening of the drey. The MacRed family now knew that the food was guaranteed right through to the spring. After a wonderful evening, they retired to the sleeping area to dream and await a new day's adventures.

The Snowball Fight

A few days later, Tim, Jenny and Angus were on their way home from school with four leverets. Although the snow had ceased to fall, the ground was still deep and heavy from the days before. They all made light footprints in the snow as they wended their way through the bushes with not a care in the world.
"What a morning! Have I got news to tell Father!" said Tim, the eldest of the three MacRed children. They had just learned from Owl that they also had another name, or a number of other names in fact, according to the zoology and biology books they had been learning from.
"Sciuridae!" shouted Tim.
"Sciurini to you!" replied Jenny.
"Sciuridae!" they all shouted together but Angus was still too young to really understand what they were talking about.
"Sciuridae, Sciurini, Sciurus vulgaris Timothy MacRed of that Ilk, if you please!" exclaimed an excited Tim to his group of friends. The leverets had still not learned their zoological names so that they felt somewhat inferior.
"What a lot of nonsense! You're just a squirrel like all the others!" they cried in defence.

As they proceeded, the leverets, feeling somewhat put out by the pompous squirrels, picked up balls of snow and threw them at the heads of the young squirrels.
"That will teach you to show off!" one of them shouted.
The squirrels jumped excitedly to one side and each of them picked up a handful of snow and moulded it into a solid ball.
"One, two, three, fire!" the three squirrels all shouted at once and the leverets took cover before returning fire. The animals danced, twisted, jumped up in the air and even somersaulted!

The fight went on for five to ten minutes and the creatures were totally absorbed in their play. Another animal, not too far away though, was totally absorbed in them. A large, lean and hungry fox had seen the footprints left by the young animals and had been following them by sight and by smell. He had heard the commotion and awaited his chance behind the bushes with the anticipation of a nice, fresh meal. Suddenly, Tim caught sight of its large, red tail and froze. He stood up on his hind legs and sniffed the air. It was a fox alright. He flicked his tail and stamped his feet so that the others would notice. Then he ran towards them and gave a shrill alarm call - a staccato bark, indicating that a ground predator was around. The animals scattered and fled for their lives as the fox rushed out of the bushes towards one of the leverets and young Angus, who was not so experienced with danger. "Seet-bark!" shouted Tim, and he and Jenny scurried up a tree trunk out of reach. There they looked down at the scene from their safe location, both flicking their tails and stamping their feet and even trying to throw down snowballs at the fox - all in vain. The leverets couldn't climb and they shot into the bushes together with Angus in search of a hiding place. Fox though was too quick and hungry and he snapped his mouth at the back legs of a leveret frantically running for its young life. Angus emitted a scream and the other squirrels a loud barking noise. Fox though tripped up the young leveret and in a swoop he was down on it with his mouth. There was nothing more the others could do now but hide. The young leveret was dead and fox looked around for a place to eat his prey.

Suzy Squirrel had heard the commotion and the alarm calls from the others as they were not too far away from the home drey. She hurried to the scene where Angus was still hiding in the bushes, scared for his life. Suzy cried to the others and soon they were re-united. They all jumped to the floor and ran after the fox in an attempt to mob and harass him away. The other leverets too knew now what to do and joined the group. Fox knew he was outnumbered and quickly left the scene, though he was not going to drop his meal and he disappeared into the bushes.
"You leverets look for a hiding place. Tim and Jenny up the tree as quickly as possible," exclaimed an anxious Suzy and she then rushed into the bushes where Angus was located.
"Seet, help," cried the forlorn youngster.
Suzy picked him up in her mouth and jumped up the tree where the others were waiting. She then gazed down at the bloody snow and the broken twigs and branches everywhere. After some five minutes of sniffing and gazing all around, she was sure that the fox had gone. She gave an all-clear call to the leverets still in hiding and they scurried off home as fast as they could to the safety of their burrow.

The four squirrels now climbed even higher and jumped hurriedly from branch to branch in the treetops to reach the safety of the drey in the hollow. The children were exhausted after all the excitement of the snowball fight and then the fox, and they fell quickly asleep on their moss and leaves. When Tipple arrived home, Suzy told him all that had happened and how Angus was nearly swallowed up. When the children were awake again, Tipple drilled them all on safety and alarm calls and made sure that Angus would know what to do the next time danger struck.

"You should never get so engrossed in something that you forget about your environment," cautioned Tipple. "Even when you're feeding or playing you must keep a lookout for predators. One of you must keep guard next time for the others. The forest is far too dangerous to forget about wildcats, foxes or humans."

Then Tipple and Suzy imitated the various alarm calls once more and told the youngsters what to do in an emergency. After all the excitement and the sadness at losing one of their friends, the children were no longer so eager to tell their parents of their newly-learned names.

"I think we'd better wait till tomorrow or the day after. I hate foxes!" said a tired and thoughtful Jenny Squirrel.

Survival Skills

It was March now and the snow had gone. Spring had come early to this part of Scotland, as it had done for a few years now, and all of nature was emerging earlier from its winter slumbers. The sun was still quite cool but everywhere there was the sign of regeneration. The buds had started to appear on the deciduous trees and the grass was sprouting forth on the forest floor. Bluebells or Gowk's thimmles, daffodils and primula were pushing their tentative way through the fresh soil. Blackbirds, song thrushes and coal tits had been joined by the first willow warblers and chiffchaffs and the forest was full of song. This warmed the heart of Tipple and his family and they enjoyed communicating in the tree canopy with their feathered friends as well as basking in the warm sunshine after the long, cold winter air.

Down below there was more activity too. Rare black grouse that had also seen out the winter were looking for fresh shoots and buds and a woodcock could be seen looking for worms. Insects too were scurrying about the forest floor, still damp from the melted snow and fresh rain.

Tipple was out and about early one morning looking for his midden of pine cones from the autumn. He knew they were near an old oak tree that he had marked with his scent but this was months ago and the scent had probably worn off. He returned to where he had met William Hedgehog and then he looked around for the oak tree. It wasn't long before he found what he thought was the right one and climbing headfirst down the trunk of the oak, he paused to keep a lookout for predators, other squirrels or jays and crows who always succeeded in finding his food when he wasn't so vigilant. Everything was clear, and he proceeded to search near to the oak. After a few minutes, he had found his treasured stock that had been buried for so long under a blanket of snow. They were still moist and nutritious and he proceeded to eat one, carefully biting through the outer shell to obtain the delicious seeds and to restore his energy needs. Suddenly, there was a noise to the left in the undergrowth. He darted up the tree trunk and at some eight feet above the ground he peered all around to see what it was.
"False alarm," he said to himself as two blackbirds scraped around in the leaves, oblivious to his cones.

He jumped back down on to the ground and decided to reorganize the cones to improve security. One already nibbled specimen though and a second one were tightly held in his mouth, one at each side like a pair of torpedoes. He ran quickly up the trunk and darted from branch to branch back to the drey with the precious cargo. On his return, Tipple was surprised to find that Tim was in bed with tummy troubles and was feeling quite forlorn. He had been eating some of the recovered acorns and Tipple ascertained that they were rather bitter, containing far too much tannin. He made up his mind to visit the summer residence some half a mile away where he had a store of mushrooms drying in the nook of a tree. These would be just the thing for Tim's stomach ache he thought, but he wanted to wait until Jenny and Angus were back from school as he had additional plans for the afternoon. He would take the two youngsters on a survival tour and at the same time see that all was right at the summer nest and bring back some mushrooms for Tim. Tipple was always the opportunist, combining activities to save time and energy and he was well-respected for his economy and thrift.

As soon as lunch was over, Tipple, Jenny and Angus set off on their journey. The first thing to teach Angus was how to climb down a tree headfirst. Showing him how he could rotate his hind feet through 180°, Tipple stretched himself out from trunk to branch and then descended the trunk of a Scots pine with ease, almost in slow motion.
"You see, it's easy! Now you try it," he called to Angus. Wee Angus was pretty scared at first but through trial and error and a good deal of observation and encouragement from his father, he quickly mastered the acrobatic moves. Jenny was eager too to show off her prowess and she not only ran down the trunk of the pine but also clung on with only her hind feet, carrying a twig in her front paws. This was too much for Angus though who was content to have even mastered the basic moves.
"This will help you to find food and to look for danger," said a proud Tipple.

At the first beech tree, Tipple couldn't resist tasting the new buds and young shoots.
"Mmm, delicious," and he offered some to the children. Soon they were at the site of the summer nest. It was still there, nestled in the fork of a Douglas fir tree and in fairly good condition after the harsh winter. Tipple thought it would only need a bit of patching up for the spring and summer months. Just above the nest was Tipple's supply of mushrooms, drying out in the warm sun.
"These are Orange-Peel fungi and these here are the Shaggy Ink-Cap. But it's this one that will make Tim well again. It's the Fly Agaric which you can recognize by its red colour and white spots when you pick it. We dry them to preserve them for later, and I'll show you some mushrooms we can eat later on in the day."

By now the mushrooms were not so colourful. Tipple explained to the children how important it was to eat different foods so as not to be dependent on one single source.

"We'll take some of this back to the drey when we return," explained Tipple to the children.

"Now when you're up here in the branches, it doesn't mean that you're out of harm's way. Always be on the look-out for pine martens throughout the year, and up in the sky there are buzzards and hawks and hoolits or owls waiting to pounce on us. If you see a hawk circling or hovering, you must hide in the leaves in the summer, and in the winter seek out a nook or cranny at once. You can also press yourself against the bark of a conifer. Because of our red fur, we cannot be seen so easily against the reddish bark. That's why we have an almost black dorsal stripe in the winter. Then you must cry out 'chuck, chuck, kwa' or 'seet bark' and stamp your feet. This will tell the hawk that you have seen him and put an end to his escapades because they rely on surprise. Never be surprised yourselves by other animals or humans, even when basking in the sun or feeding. It could mean your end!"

"Then you need to keep on the look-out before coming out of your hiding place. When it's all clear, you can continue carefully on your way but you should always use similar routes and know where your hiding places are for a quick getaway."

Trying to survive!

The three of them now scrambled down to the forest floor and gathered old leaves and moss for the nest repairs. These they put into a neat, little pile and then Tipple proceeded to warn the youngsters about wildcats that could also climb trees, whilst at the same time using his large, front teeth to strip some bark off a Spruce tree.

"We can use this to line the nest as well," he explained.

They then darted up a tree again and sprang from branch to branch to enter deeper into the forest. Here it was darker as the still weak sun had not penetrated through the dense cluster of pine trees. There on the damp forest floor was Mother Nature's larder for squirrels - a host of succulent mushrooms. Tipple showed the kits the edible Orange-Peel that looked like its namesake, and a little further were the Shaggy Ink-Caps.

"This one's bell-shaped, white and covered with scales like a fish, so it's easy to identify. We can dry and eat this one as well. In fact, squirrels and mushrooms go together like dogs and fleas. We can eat mushrooms that other animals and humans can't, and they provide us with lots of water, potassium and copper to strengthen our immune system against diseases. There's one though that we can't eat as it's very poisonous for us too - the Death Cap. Here, it's practically all-white with a greenish cap."

As they darted here and there in nervous excitement, Tipple chanced upon a rare find. First making sure that all was clear, he brought Jenny and Angus to an antler from one of the forest's stags.

"What a treat!" exclaimed Tipple, but Jenny and Angus were quite puzzled and wondering how their father was going to eat it.

"This is a squirrel's dream-come-true," he told the children. "First, by gnawing on the bone we can wear down and sharpen our front teeth. If you don't do this, my word, you'll end up all teeth and no food! Secondly, you can swallow some calcium, vital for teeth and bones of adults and young folk alike. Here, come and get a well-earned nibble whilst I keep a lookout. Simply delicious!"

As Tipple looked around, he heard some familiar chatter in the trees above. Looking up, who should he see but two of his friends, Forrest and Dalbeattie Squirrel, also out and about looking for food and nesting material. They too were red squirrels and they lived in another part of the forest. After greeting one another by rubbing their faces together and briskly brandishing their tails, Tipple and Forrest Squirrel caught up on the latest news.

"How did you survive the winter?" asked a concerned Tipple.

"Through my cache of beech nuts and acorns and the midden of pine cones, like you I suppose," explained Forrest, "but there was a constant supply of free food from the humans too!"

Tipple eagerly pricked up his ears in anticipation.

"On the edge of the forest, near us, we discovered some cottages with a garden, and on one tree the people have hung out nuts, seeds and even fruit for the birds. If you keep watch for a pesky black and white moggy, getting to the food is a piece of cake. The humans think the blackbirds and sparrows have such great appetites and every day there's a feast!"

"How far is it from here?" asked an excited Tipple.

"About ten minutes through the firs," replied Forrest Squirrel.

Tipple thought this would be good training for the youngsters to take part in a daylight garden raid and after jumping back on to the branches they were soon on their way.

Forrest Squirrel

Ten, hectic minutes later and somewhat out of breath, they arrived at the clearing where a row of cottages with neat but natural gardens waited below. Tipple and Forrest tested out the territory, felt that it was quiet enough and gave the all-clear to Dalbeattie, Jenny and Tim to follow. They were soon at the gardens and five impudent faces peered through the garden fence. The feeders were still hung in the trees and although somewhat depleted by the birds, there were still rich pickings. The children were egged on to jump on to the overhanging tree and watched by the cautious adults, the kits proceeded to gorge themselves on sunflower seeds, unsalted peanuts and oat flakes. Whilst Tipple kept a lookout, Forrest and Dalbeattie made their way to the flower beds. Squeezing through the wooden fence, the bushy-tailed perpetrators started to dig up some newly-planted geraniums and begonias and to munch on the petals and roots. Then it was on to the vegetable garden with a dig for carrots and parsley. Tipple decided it would be a good idea to take some carrots back with him for the family as they were very nutritious, whilst the parsley was good for cleaning the teeth.

Suddenly they were spotted! A large gentleman hurried out of the cottage shouting "Awa' wi' ye, ye scoundrels!" and started to throw objects that were close at hand at the marauding band. The man was followed by a Westie terrier that liked nothing better than to chase a group of mischievous rodents. Within a flash, the squirrels were down the tree and out of the garden and running for their lives through the fence and to the safety of the forest. It had once again been a perilous encounter with humans, but Tipple had one and a half carrots (he had just swallowed a half of one when the alarm bells rang) still in his grasp, everyone had eaten their fill and the kits had seen some real enemies again. The garden they left behind though was slightly reminiscent of trench warfare on a good day.

"A real watering hole," gasped Tipple, once more in the safety of a tree branch, "but a little bit hairy. The humans have good eyes too."
As pleased as Punch with their exploits, they all scampered back along the tree tops taking the same route that they came. Forrest and Dalbeattie Squirrel bade farewell to the others after nearing their drey, but they all

agreed they would meet up again soon. Tipple then led Jenny and Angus back to the summer nest where the children were each given a dry Fly Agaric to carry back home for Tim. Tipple made a mental note again of the required repairs, then it was time to return to the beech tree and the security of the drey.

"Quite a catch!" observed Tipple. "Mother will be proud of us after all that we've done and have brought home."

When they got back to the drey though, Suzy Squirrel was somewhat distraught. Tim had decided to go and look himself for some herbs for his stomach ache, and that was hours ago. He hadn't returned.

An Encounter with the MacGrey's

It was almost dark now and still there was no sign of Tim. They were all very worried especially as he was also ill, but Tipple decided it would be too dangerous to look for him now in the dark. Not only would it be perilous in the branches, there were too many owls and other night predators with much better eyesight in the darkness. Where could Tim have got to?

The next morning after Jenny and Angus were off to school, Tipple and Suzy started out to look for Tim in the forest. First they scampered across the treetops but after some time they felt it would be wiser to check the forest floor in case Tim had fallen. At Aithouse Burn, Suzy sprang across the water but Tipple jumped in head first and swam to the other side - he somehow thought he must check the water too, and after all it was an emergency. Once on terra firma again, he shook off the excess water droplets and they carried on their search making frequent chirping calls as they went. There was no sign of Tim though and they decided to call on Benjamin Badger to see if he had seen their eldest son. Badger was also out and about near to his sett looking for fresh insects and roots.
"Good morning to you, Tipple and Suzy," he declared.
"Oh, it's not a good morning today," explained Tipple. "We've lost our Tim since yesterday lunchtime when he left the drey with tummy problems to look for some herbs. We haven't seen him since."
"Neither have I," said a concerned Badger, "but I can help you look for him on the ground. It's not safe for squirrels down here what with wildcats, foxes, pine martens and the like. I'd keep to the branches if I were you!"
"Good idea!" replied Tipple and after a swish of his tail, he and Suzy were back up in the pines and fresh, green deciduous trees. They went to the summer nest, the midden, the clearing and the edge of the forest where they were obliged to check the main road leading to Hawick.
There was no sign of a dead or injured squirrel, but plenty of cars and lorries and a dead rabbit or two and Tipple and Suzy had to refrain themselves from dashing across the tarmac to check the other side. Up above them there was a sparrow hawk circling and it was time to return to the branches.

Back in the forest, they asked the chaffinches, who were always gossiping about something and knew all the news about everyone, if they had seen Tim. Not a sign. As they became more and more worried, they saw a large midden down on the forest floor. They climbed down the sycamore tree and inspected the hoard. Using his sense of smell, Tipple ascertained that it was not a red squirrel's. Suddenly, there was a loud cry behind them from an irate creature.

"Keep yer thieving paws awa from ma nuts! They're all mine!"

Tipple and Suzy were so taken by surprise that they nearly jumped out of their fur and they started back up the tree trunk.

"Ah, it's you, Tipple. What are ye doing in this part of the woods, not afta' my nuts, I hope?!"

It was a grey squirrel, camouflaged against a silver birch tree. He was perfectly groomed, somewhat larger than Tipple and Suzy, with a menacing voice and a stamping foot. His eyes were large and his tail was much thinner but curved up over his back like an Egyptian fan. As he talked, he was still chewing on a spinnin' jenny that he had caught by chance on the bark of the birch. The midden he was defending was neat and orderly with rows of old pine cones, rows of beech nuts and a row of half-buried seeds. This squirrel was clearly very organized and was a larder-hoarder as well as a scatter-hoarder. It was in fact one known to Tipple and he was soon joined by two other small greys that were his offspring.

"Good day to you, Sandy MacGrey!" said a somewhat perturbed Tipple, not knowing how they were going to react to this intrusion. "We are looking for our son, Tim MacRed, and we thought he might have strayed in the forest as he's not too well."

Tipple and Sandy MacGrey had met before so they were acquaintances, but our hero was somewhat cautious. He had warned the family to avoid grey squirrels at all costs as he knew they were passive carriers of the dreaded parapox virus which had killed off a number of his red-furred friends. For that reason, he and Suzy kept their distance as they communicated with their North American cousins.

"No, we've no' seen any reds in this neck o' the woods in the last few days, but have some of ma nuts. Ye must be awful hungry if you've been searchin' all day!"

Sandy MacGrey sprang down the tree and with a leap and a bound he was at the side of the birch tree. There he started to dig frantically in a cache and pulled up four or five acorns.

"These a' red acorns and very tasty. I know you reds canna abide them normally as they taste a wee bit bitter. Well, I pulled out the embryo in the autumn and then buried them so they're no so bitter. Here, try one!"

"I'd like to," replied Tipple who was awful hungry, but he didn't dare risk the pox.

"We'll join you another time, if you don't mind. We have to carry on our search for our son."

Tipple and Suzy were soon on their way again and they stopped for a drink and a bite to eat after all. Tipple sunk his incisors into a Norway Spruce and he and Suzy nibbled their way through the pieces of bark. After that they were able to eat the sweet and succulent phloem tissue underneath and then take a refreshing drink of the sap.

Once again they continued their search, but to no avail. Tired and despondent, they met up again with Benjamin Badger who had also been far and wide but there was not a trace of the young squirrel. They decided to return to the drey to meet up with Jenny and Angus and to tell them the news that they had lost their brother. The four squirrels were about to sit down and console themselves with a meal of pine seeds and a carrot when there was a shuffling noise at the entrance to the drey. Tipple emitted a "kuk" sound as he expected a predator but it was nothing of the sort. Tim was back at the drey somewhat exhausted, hungry and bedraggled and with a shaved tail and sides.

The family were all so pleased to see him alive and after welcoming him back they gave him some water and seeds and a piece of mushroom. Then they all sat down to a real meal for an explanation of what had happened.
"I left the drey yesterday lunchtime," recounted Tim. "I thought I would get some herbs or mushrooms for my stomach ache. Well, when I was down on the forest floor there was a swishing sound and then I couldn't see anything. I jumped here and there, wiggled and squirmed to try and escape but there was simply no way out. I had been caught in a net by some humans. The only thing I remember was being picked up in the net and then being taken in a car to somewhere not too far away, but I was very scared. They then took me into one of their houses, and removing the net, one of the humans held me tight whilst another approached me brandishing some fiendish contraption. I thought I was for it, but they only wanted to shave my tail and rear. The cheek of it! I tried to squirm and bite them of course but to no avail. The dirty deed had been done. Then, this morning, I was put in a sort of box with openings for air and a bit of light, and then they brought me back to the forest in a car. I remember hoping that it was our forest.

Well, they then put the box on the ground and opened the door of the box. I hesitated for a moment as I thought it was one of their tricks, but they walked away and I took my chance to flee and scurried up the nearest tree. After getting my breath back, I started to look for our drey but couldn't find it and wandered around helplessly for a time. Then I met of all things a jay who proudly stated that he knew not only where our drey was but also our cache of nuts. He kindly led me through the branches to our home and here I am!"

"What an adventure!" stated Tipple. "These humans are a menace. You know why they caught you? They're after our bushy tails, particularly the long, lateral hairs and do you know what for? They use them for artists' brushes. Imagine. Brushes! The indignity of it all! But never mind, young Tim, they let you go again and you're alive and well and back with us. Even if you do look a bit like a scarecrow at present, your tail will grow again before the summer when you can use it again to protect against the sun. In the meantime though, I'd avoid the narrow branches if I were you, as you're lost there without a tail to balance you. We don't want you falling and breaking a leg or something on top of all this!"

The squirrels laughed and were mighty relieved to have the family all together again. After dinner, the younger children did some preparation for school the next day and Tipple and Suzy, somewhat exhausted after all the day's ups and downs, relaxed and fell asleep on the cool moss.

A Wedding Day

It was mid-summer now and the MacRed's were enjoying the warmth, extra light and the plentiful supply of food. The larder was practically bursting, the summer residence had been repaired by the whole family and they were often to be seen staying the night there instead of returning to the drey. The summer nest was more airy and cool than the winter drey and the children especially liked the "beds" made of grass and straw in the tree forks that they were all able to sleep in. The nest was located high up in a Douglas Fir between three diverging branches and there was a sort of lookout area at the front where they could look down on the forest habitat and peer up to the cloudless, blue sky.

The forest was full of bird song - Tipple could hear the tree pippits, the warblers, the goldcrests and the crossbills all busy searching for nourishment for their young. A nightjar too had made its nest not too far away and the air was filled with hoverflies, midges, red-necked footman moths and pearl-bordered fritillary butterflies. Purple foxgloves were in full bloom along with geraniums and white ramsons and there was thick foliage in the trees ensuring plenty of camouflage for the squirrels from predators. It was the time of year that Tipple enjoyed the most but it was also his busiest time.

Little did he know how busy! Suzy Squirrel was estrous again – ready to breed - and Tipple had his hands full to keep all the other squirrels, lured by the intoxicating odour, away from the nest. Suzy had to stay indoors for the time being, but there were plenty of young bachelors waiting their chance nearby to catch Tipple and Suzy unawares and to take part in a mating chase. Tipple knew their game though and had received a number of scars in the past together with patches of bald fur to prove it! This time he was keeping guard and he would let no squirrel pass. By the afternoon, most of the other males had lost interest anyway and were keen to attend to their hunger and cache activities before returning to their own homes, but every morning it was the same game with the other reds trying to lure Tipple and Suzy out of their fortification.

When all the hullaballoo had died down, Tipple set out to find some fresh food, accompanied by all three children this time. He thought it was time to give them some more survival tips and to give Suzy a rest at home.
"Only female cones contain the seeds we need and these are rich in magnesium and protein," said Tipple to the attentive children. "Only the male cones contain pollen. The cones we want are found high up at the end of the

branches and you have to be pretty agile to get at them. They're at their best in the autumn. On the Sitka Spruce and the Norway Spruce trees there's also a sort of trick of nature - a pseudo-cone. This is called pineapple gall which looks rather like a cone from the distance, but it's only a catkin and has no nutritional value. When you find a cone, you need to get your front teeth round the stem and sever it from the branch. Then, never forget to look out for enemies when opening and chewing. The faster you can get at the seeds and go on to the next cone or tree the better. Remember, we need a quick and rich source of energy for all our jumping about and it's not too bad to put on a bit of weight for the winter!"

"What else can we eat? At this time of year there are tasty, crunchy grasshoppers, buds, flowers, apples, beetles, butterflies, caterpillars and if you're lucky a few birds' eggs but you have to be quick here as the mother bird is never far away and has a sharp beak! The forest is also the place for mushrooms - we need to collect these and dry them in a tree for the winter months and in the autumn there are delicious truffles. These are found in clusters under the soil and the best way to find them is to smell and dig! They smell very strong, slightly garlicky. Then we have to plan ahead for the winter. Late summer, early autumn is the time for nuts - walnuts, chestnuts, beech nuts, hazelnuts and acorns. Walnuts are simply wonderful, full of copper and iron and unsaturated fatty acids - this means we can digest them much more quickly. It's better to bury them with their shells as then they don't germinate and they have a slightly barriquey taste like in an oak barrel. Mmm! Acorns though are a problem."

At this point, Tipple took the youngsters to the cache of acorns and dug up a few.
"You see there are white oak acorns and red oak acorns and as our grey squirrel friend showed us, if they germinate - which they do quite quickly in the ground - then they're less nutritious. The trick is to remove the embryos with your teeth and then bury them so they can't germinate. The red-oak acorns are somewhat high in tannins which make them bitter, as Tim found out to his cost, so if you can stick to the white ones all the better."

"How do you tell the difference between white oaks and red oaks?" asked Tim, not wanting to have tummy ache again.
"The white oak leaves are rounded at the tops and have no bristles on the tips like the red oaks," explained his father. "Any other questions?"
"Yes," said Angus, "How do you open a nut? I can't get them out of their hard shells."

"That's easy. Hold the nut in your front paws, brace it with your upper front teeth and rasp it with your lower ones. When you've made a hole, then enlarge this with the lower incisors. Then you can reach the nut which you can grind with your molars! Time is important. Never get so engrossed with your nut that you forget where you are."

Once the lesson in things to eat was completed, Tipple took the youngsters back to the summer nest and they practised gathering the materials to re-make the nest.
"In the forest, there's everything we need for a comfortable home," and they started to gather twigs and damp leaves. "This is for the wall structure," said Tipple, and he showed the children how to put them together.
"We use moss for the base as it's nice and soft and we line the walls with stripped bark, moss, moulting fur and anything that's soft or fluffy left over by the humans. It should be a circular nest high up in a tree fork with a good view of the territory and be at least three or four feet in diameter for a family."
"I want to learn how to build a bed!" cried Angus, but Tipple felt that was enough learning for today.

The youngsters went off to play in the vicinity of the summer home and Tipple returned to the nest to be greeted by Suzy with very fresh news.
"Guess who's getting married?" she asked.
"I've no idea," replied a slightly disinterested Tipple.
"Why, Forrest and Dalbeatties' eldest daughter, and we've been invited this Saturday!"
This was good news for Suzy who liked to interact with their red neighbours but it was not such good news for Tipple who thought about all the extra preparation involved - a present, looking spick and span, getting the children ready, getting everyone there on time...Tipple sought the refuge of his bed. There he tried to think about a present. It had to be something special. Then he had a brainwave - it was time to visit the humans at the cottages again!

The next day they all set off bright and early to the forest cottages with the wonderful gardens. It was a very hot day and Tipple and the family were quite worn out when they arrived at the gardens again. Where they had been with Forrest had all been repaired but there were no bird feeders this time, only a table with some seeds and nuts. What Tipple really had his eye on though was in the next garden, which had a lawn. There in full flow was a garden sprinkler watering the grass.
"A great opportunity for a shower!" exclaimed Tipple. "Everyone under the water at once before they see us. It will get rid of the ticks and mites and freshen us up for the wedding!"

Angus and Tipple stood on one side of the contraption and Suzy, Tim and Jenny on the other and they were soon jumping about in the alternate showers of water. After everyone was thoroughly wet, they shook themselves like a dog and waited for the sun to dry them. Tipple was particularly keen to restore his tufts and tail to their original form and splendour.
Then it was on to the original garden. Tipple couldn't resist the bird food on the open table but as he munched on the first seeds he had a shock.
"Yuk!" cried Tipple and spat out the offending food. "What a cheek! They've put cayenne pepper on it to stop us squirrels from eating." With that he returned quickly to the next garden and swilled and gargled with the water from the sprinkler to get rid of the exotic, spicy taste.

Rejoining the others and slightly peeved, Tipple had other plans though. "Everyone on to the greenhouse roof," he shouted and the five marauders were slipping about on the sloping glass and making their way to a slightly open window. Squeezing and wiggling through the gap, they sprang on to the tomato plants.
"A perfect present for the wedding couple," exclaimed Tipple and he pulled off two large, ripe tomatoes. Giving one to Suzy, they gripped the fruits in their mouth and jumped back up to the open window. This was easier said than done for Angus and even Jenny had problems reaching the window, but with a little help above from Tipple and below from their mother, they all made it back on to the roof. Then they jumped across to an apple tree and over the wooden fence and then it was a quick dash to the safety of the forest again. "Mission accomplished!" thought Tipple. He had successfully groomed the whole family and acquired the wedding present.

Once they were home, Suzy placed the two tomatoes in a straw nest and added a few petals for decoration. The wedding took place a couple of days later on a warm and sunny day in the secret clearing. Badger was presiding in his usual officious way and there were all the animals there that can trust each other including Owl the schoolteacher - deer, other red squirrels, rabbits and hares, beavers, a whole range of our feathered friends except the carnivores, a badger friend of Benjamin Badger, quite a few weasels, and of course the proud Forrest and Dalbeattie Squirrel and their lovely daughter Tibby Squirrel. She was bright and bushy-tailed with a perfectly groomed glossy, red fur. On her head and neck she was decorated with a garland of blue, woodland forget-me-nots and yellow dyer's broom and she looked even cuter than normal! Her husband-to-be was a young red squirrel called Toby Trotternish Squirrel, an athletic, muscular red who had recently inherited four middens and a number of caches from his uncle which made him a very eligible bachelor, though this of course is not a prerequisite for marrying in the squirrel world. He was a handsome fellow with exquisitely groomed and moistened ear tufts and a bright, shiny red coat. Each of the future partners was carrying a pine cone in their left paw and an oak leaf in the right one. Badger conducted the ceremony waving a silver birch branch to and fro and

In my Sunday best for the wedding day

after the couple had committed themselves to each other, there was a great feast of forest goodies that had been prepared for the guests - seeds, buds, flowers, nuts, grass, dried insects and mushrooms and a number of branches and telephone cables to gnaw on.

After the ceremony was over, Tipple and his family bade farewell to the other animals and returned to the summer nest to sleep off all the fine fare.

Lumberjacks!

It was soon late summer and all the animals were busy feeding themselves up for the winter and making a stock for the cold months. Tipple was no exception, and to the sound of larks high up in the sky, waxwings and crested tits in the treetops and with a loud humming noise of bees and other insects, he was on one of his usual rounds to find food. There was no lack of that at this time of the year and for the opportunist squirrel there was always something left behind on the benches or in the refuse bins by the many humans that were now entering the forest daily for recreation and picnics. Tipple knew instinctively that he had to eat at least a third of his body weight plus a little more for the winter, but he was keen to avoid a mid-life paunch which would reduce his athleticism and ability to escape from predators. He was thus very careful not to eat too much or to be caught off guard.

The summer flowers were beautiful at this time of the year and apart from the evergreens, the forest was a blanket of thick, green leaves providing plenty of cover. Even the forest floor was bright and cheery with the strong sun penetrating the forest glades. Tipple was deep into the forest when suddenly he heard a loud whirring and chopping sound together with humans shouting loudly. He froze for a moment to assess the danger and then made his way across the branches towards the sounds which were getting louder and louder by the minute.

There were humans right enough with trucks and chain saws and thick, orange ropes - loggers! Tipple peered down from a neighbouring spruce and saw that the fir trees were being felled one after another. "Timber!" rang out the cry of the loggers as they then trimmed the trees of their branches and loaded the logs on to great trucks to carry off to the saw-mill. It made Tipple very unsettled as he saw his food supply dwindling so quickly and he began to stamp his feet and swish his tail in irritation. The noise was deafening to him and he could see that the humans too were wearing something to cover their ears and eyes. It seemed that they were proceeding in a straight line as it were, and this was very unusual to Tipple. In fact, there hadn't been any activity of this sort for at least two years now which made it all the more unusual. He decided it was time to make a retreat and inform the family of what was happening - after all, it wasn't too far away from their summer nest.

When Tipple got back to the summer home though, the nest was no longer there! In fact the tree along with several others was no longer there, nor was Suzy! The loggers had been earlier in the morning and had already felled the Douglas Firs. Tipple wandered over to the pile of branches left behind on the floor and found a distraught Suzy Squirrel trying to rescue some items from the desolation. The summer nest was more or less completely in ruins and there was no sign of life anymore! Collecting a handful of dried mushrooms, they made their way back up to the relative safety of the higher branches and decided to return to the winter drey.

After some fifteen minutes of hectic jumping and wriggling, the two arrived at the drey. It was still intact thank goodness and Tipple gave a sigh of relief. When the children came home from school that afternoon, they had even more disturbing news for the stunned parents. Owl had heard that the lumberjacks were there to make the way clear for a road directly through the forest heading north and the children were of course eager to pass on the news.
"A road?!" cried Tipple, and he thought of the many dangers and intrusion that would bring - cars, trucks, motorcycles, noise, roadkill, more tourists!
He was not sure if he could believe the children though and he decided to make a visit to Badger to ascertain whether this was true or not.

"Sure enough!" exclaimed Badger, who was very worried about the forest being divided into two parts and the problem of getting from one part to the other safely. "You're okay, Tipple. You can jump across the trees but folk like me and the deer and rabbits will have a hard time of it. Dear me, dear me, I don't know what we're going to do!"

"We'd better get together with Owl and the others as soon as possible and decide what we can do," suggested Tipple. Benjamin Badger agreed with an air of resignation.

Two days went by and Tipple had arranged a meeting for the animals in the clearing the next day. Whilst Tipple was out together with Suzy on a feeding, scattering and reconnaissance trip in the area of the woodcutters, the latter had begun to work in the other direction to the south-west and the forest was filled with the sound of sawing and cutting. From the canopy of the forest, Tipple had almost a bird's-eye view of the proceedings and could see where the humans had cut a swath through the trees. They were even cutting down the mature and majestic beech and sycamore trees on which the animals relied for their food and hiding places. After gathering some cones and a few tasty insects, the two made their way back to their drey.

Tipple was in for another shock. The beech tree had been cut down together with other deciduous neighbours and the workmen had left a trail of destruction.
"Our lovely drey!" exclaimed Suzy in despair.
"Our lovely larder!" replied an equally despondent Tipple.
On closer inspection they found too that all the drey's contents had fallen out and that "intruders" had been taking advantage of the easy pickings. In fact, not far away, a group of jays and crows were also digging up and feeding on one of Tipple's caches. This was clearly not one of Tipple's best weeks.

They promptly decided to pick up the children from the school and to bring the meeting of the animals in the clearing forward as soon as possible. That very evening, just before it got dark and all felt reasonably safe, the animals gathered in the forest clearing where they usually met. The hares and the deer were particularly stressed and shaking their heads in despair as Tipple and family arrived on the scene. Everyone was quiet and curious as to what Owl and Badger would have to say. The woodcutters had of course long since left the forest and all was calm and peaceful once again. The blackbirds and linnets were still up in the trees making their last calls of the day to establish their territories before retiring to the safety of their roosts. Many bird such as the nightingales, the redstarts, the woodpeckers and the treecreepers were also present at the proceedings as they too were eager to hear what they could do to protect their habitat and food source.

"There are just two possibilities," explained Badger. "We can either disrupt the work a little or we can just accept the new situation. Either way, we won't be able to stop the humans, that's a fact." Owl agreed. The birds were not quite so worried about the new road as they could fly over it, but they were concerned about the noise of traffic disrupting their bird calls.
"We'll just have to sing louder!" said one of the nightingales.
"Why don't we all lie down on the new road when it starts to be built and pretend to be roadkill!" suggested one of the hares with a flash of ingenuity. "In that way, the humans will think that if so many animals die on the first day, then they won't want to continue the building work."
"I don't think they'll fall for that!" said an exasperated Badger. "Maybe we should demonstrate like the humans do when they don't want something! No seriously, we must come to a decision as to what we're going to do. Our lives and well-being are at stake!"

Tipple and Suzy were partly concentrating on the discussion and partly on their housing dilemma.

"What if we re-build the drey and then the next tree gets cut down, and how are we to get across the road and look for food safely?" mused a thoughtful Tipple.

The animals were not used to human intrusion on this scale, and Tipple had more or less made up his mind to move on and look for a quieter spot further north. The hares decided that they would remain at Craik Forest and see how things developed in the truest sense of the word. Owl and the birds were going to stay too as they could easily expand their habitat into the nearby fields and meadows. Badger was not so flexible and the incident with the dog had clearly unsettled him.
"Humans, humans, humans wherever you go! It never used to be like this in the old days. My grandfather told me that animals like us never saw a human unless we left the forest or unless there was a hunt, and then we could always find a safe hiding place. I'm for moving on," he reluctantly admitted.

Tipple and Suzy explained to the group that they would be seeking a new habitat as well and they made plans with Forrest and Dalbeattie Squirrel and Badger to set off northwards as soon as possible. The other animals were too shy and inexperienced to risk going across country to find a new home and they would stay at Craik.

That night Tipple and his family slept in the fork of a fir tree near to the old summer home. Fortunately, it was summer and there was plenty to eat and the evenings were warm and pleasant. They fell asleep clearly thinking of all they had to do and plan.

Part Two

On to Glentress Forest

The next day was a typical summer's day with the sound of siskins and warblers, buzzing insects and small creatures such as mice and voles scampering through the undergrowth in search of food. Tipple had only been awake an hour or so and was also ready to go out on a food sortie. Suddenly, there was the nearby sound of trucks and workmen approaching. Then the deafening noise of chain saws working in unison to fell more trees for the coming road construction.
"That's it!" exclaimed a clearly upset Tipple. "A squirrel can't even start the day in peace anymore!"

Collecting the family together, they all set off to Badger's sett to meet up with Forrest and Dalbeattie. They made their way safely across the tree tops to Benjamin Badger's, leaving behind them the drone of the saws and the clamour of hectic activity in the forest. As they arrived, it was relatively quiet where Badger was and it was hard to imagine that a swath of destruction was being cut through another part of the forest. Forrest and Dalbeattie were already there and Badger had kindly provided some goodies for his squirrel guests - some bark, some pine cones and some fresh shoots. Badger himself had just finished a nourishing breakfast of insects and roots.

"Good morning dear friends!" said Badger as he popped his head out of the entrance to his sett. "We have a lot to plan today and I've brought out one of my walking maps of the district left behind by some of the human tourists - very useful for finding your way."

The eight animals sat down in front of the sett to plan their journey. Badger had worked out that from Craik Forest to Peebles in the north it was about 30 miles, give or take a mile or two. They would look for a suitable home on the way. Badger saw a large green area east of Peebles and he thought this might be a forest. The kits were very excited by all this planning and the thought of freedom and adventure. For Tipple it was a headache. Badger explained that they should set off as soon as possible and travel by night to avoid detection by humans or predators as they would have to travel over open countryside.
"What's a predator?" asked an inquisitive Angus.

"It's a bird or animal bigger than you or me and it's intent on eating you for supper if it gets the chance," explained Forrest Squirrel, winking at the same time to Angus's father.

"We shouldn't forget the humans," added Badger, "they can be predators too."

"Why would humans want to eat me?" inquired Angus.

"Because they can!" added Forrest in an attempt to frighten the young squirrel a little. This only led to Angus asking more questions.

"I'll tell you all about humans when we're travelling north," explained Tipple who was more intent on planning what they were to take with them and how they were going to find food. Badger was keen to take along his books more than anything and he would carry these in a large hemp sack found at the farm together with food for at least three days. He estimated that if they travelled at night and rested during the day, they would reach the green area in about a week. Tipple was keen to pick up some cones and collect some dry mushrooms for the family from the old summer nest, if he could still find any, before they set off, and everyone apart from Angus would have to carry something. They decided to set off that very night meeting together again at Badger's soon-to-be-deserted sett.

During the day, Tipple was busy collecting what remained on the floor from his dry mushroom stock and bringing them up to the fork in the Douglas fir tree where they had spent the night. He was also able to pick up some cones and a bit of bark with succulent tissue underneath for moisture for the journey. He hoped though that they would find a burn or two along the way. After a small rest high up in the relative safety of the fir tree, they waited for the darkness to set in.

It was a strange feeling for Tipple and Suzy as they left the comfort of their fir tree and set out carrying food in their mouths but not knowing what to expect and where their new home would be. They arrived at Badger's and he was ready with his sack and some small straw bags for the squirrels to carry their food more easily. Forrest and Dalbeattie arrived some ten minutes later, somewhat out of breath having had to make a dash behind and then up a tree to avoid a hungry tawny owl.

"Nothing like a bit of exercise and excitement to keep you awake and on your toes, or should I say claws," stated a confident Forrest.

Clutching his map of the Borders, Badger started out with the squirrels following energetically behind.

"Safety in numbers," explained Badger and soon the eight creatures were making their way through the forest along one of Badger's well-known trails.

It wasn't long before they reached the edge of the forest and here they had to be particularly vigilant as soon they would be out in the open. Tipple climbed up a nearby tree in the semi-darkness. It was not difficult for this practised squirrel. Scuttling along a large branch and using his tail to feel his way along, he stopped to sniff the air and to hear any unsettling sounds. All was quiet and looking out as best he could to the forest periphery and the barley field beyond there was hardly a stir.

"All clear!" he told the others as he rejoined the group. After leaving the forest, they crossed a strip of wasteland and then they disappeared into the barley field. After some twenty minutes, they had reached the other side and Tipple and the other squirrels were quite glad as they were not used to this type of vegetation. As they left the darkness of the barley field, the almost full moon lit up the grassland and silhouetted the small group of creatures against the forest. Suzy looked longingly behind at Craik Forest. She soon regained her composure though. There was nothing for it but to set out and find another habitat. Craik Forest would never be the same again for them.

The next day after covering some three or four miles in the night, they were all mighty tired and hungry. They all sat down in some hawthorn bushes to eat a hearty breakfast and to rest their tired legs and eyes until it got dark again. One of the adults each took it in turns to stay awake and to watch out for any dangers but luckily there were none. As soon as they had rested fully and darkness was approaching, they made themselves ready for another journey through the night. Badger was able to find the way north by observing the sunset and by following the stars and his instincts, and the animals were accompanied by a full moon that night giving them a clear view of where they were going.

"Wait!" whispered Badger, and he motioned to the others to find some cover.
"What is it?" asked a nervous Tipple.
"There's a fox on the prowl just ahead of us. If he sees or scents us, we'll have to make a run for it."
Tipple and Forrest looked around for trees but there weren't any. It was open countryside and they followed Badger in keeping still and close to the ground. They waited an anxious ten minutes. Badger saw that the fox was still there looking for food but after another ten minutes it was gone. The animals raised themselves up, Tipple erecting himself on his hind legs to get a better view. The fox had clearly left the vicinity and was to be seen heading in the direction of a small farm. They decided it was safe enough to move on again, and they carried on without further hindrance through the long night.

When day broke, the animals had come to a small burn and they decided to again make use of some nearby bushes to spend their rest time. They were able too to freshen up in the cool, bubbling, fresh water and to take a well-earned drink. They had covered some five miles that night according to Badger's calculations and he volunteered to take the first watch after a refreshing bathe in the burn.

The next night was soon upon them and they set off across fields of maize and barley. The children thought it would be a good idea to munch on some corn or barley heads as they were somewhat hungry.
"Don't do that!" shouted Tipple in alarm to his kits. "They've probably been sprayed with pesticide, which means if we eat them or even insects that have been feeding on them, we can get a really upset stomach. I've heard of many an animal dying from them."
"What's a pesticide?" asked Angus in a state of shock.
Tipple thought it was time to inform his youngest son of the dangers of human contact.
"Well, to the humans, you're a pest," he began, "and an 'icide' is a chemical made by humans to get rid of pests like you although they're really after the insects that want to feed on the crops. If you eat one of the insects after it has fed on the cereals, you'll certainly get a mighty sore tummy! The humans spray almost all the food they grow now with pesticides and they think it won't harm them. I don't know about that, but there is a saying, 'a little goes a long way.' Humans don't plan in the long term like we do. They decide on something and then do it without thinking of the dangers for other animals or even for themselves. That's why it's best not to copy them but to rely on our instincts and the practical wisdom that we adults can pass on to our children. It has worked for centuries and generations and you can't harm Mother Nature and get away with it. The humans have created their agriculture, where there are no trees or bushes anymore, just fields and fields of cereals like barley, rye or wheat. It might look pretty, but it's just like a plant called 'belladonna' which looks pretty too but is very poisonous. For we animals, it's a good place to hide until the farmer comes with his harvester or tractor and then it's just a desert where no animal can live safely anymore."

"Other things we have to watch out for are called animal predators and these include the foxes, pine martens, large birds like the owls and the hawks and the eagles, wild and domestic cats, and even some weasels."

Angus was very impressed and proud of his new vocabulary which now included two new, long words. They had managed another five miles or so when dawn began to break and in the twilight they looked around for a suitable rest. This time they found a group of beech trees and the squirrels soon found a restful spot in the foliage. Badger lay down against the trunk of the tree that the others had ascended and very soon they were all asleep after the strenuous night.

It wasn't long though before their idyll was disturbed. Around late morning when they were fast asleep, a dog let loose on a country walk with its master had scented Badger, and very soon after following its nose, it spotted him at the foot of the tree. Although the dog, a Newfoundland, was some fifty yards away, it instinctively began barking hectically and set out on the chase. Badger was awake in an instant and given a terrible fright. He had nowhere to hide and ran off towards the other trees pursued by the dog which was intent on catching him. After all the commotion, the squirrels were also awake and saw the predicament that their friend was in. Tipple and Forrest ran down the trunk of the beech tree, but without putting themselves in danger they didn't know what to do.

"There's a rope in my sack," called out an anxious Badger. "Help me climb the tree!"

Tipple raced down to the ground, opened the sack and reached in for the strong rope. Typical Badger! He always had something for emergencies. Tipple then raced up the trunk again and tied the rope over the lowest, large branch. Badger ran to the beech tree, hotly pursued by the Newfoundland, and clutching the end of the rope on the ground he shot up the tree with the aid of the rope faster than a squirrel and perched himself on the branch. The dog though was not going to give up so easily and began jumping up at the base of the beech tree. Tipple encouraged them all to pull off some branches and throw them at the dog - still to no avail. It was only when Forrest hit on the idea of throwing a branch away from the dog that it was distracted and went off to sniff what had been thrown. It wasn't as interesting as chasing a badger though and it was about to return when its master whistled for it to come back. Caught between two allurements, the dog eventually decided to obey, and reluctantly left the startled animals in peace.

"I think one of us should keep watch again!" exclaimed Badger having regained his composure somewhat. "I can't keep climbing trees like that again!"

Tipple took first watch and the other animals returned somewhat reluctantly to their slumbers. It wasn't long before dusk again fell and the animals got ready to continue their journey. They encountered no further dangers on the way and apart from a food sortie one morning to maintain their energy levels, they proceeded at a rapid pace.

Badger had been right with his prognosis. The animals reached the green area on Badger's map after six long nights. It was a large forest and as Tipple raced up a tree to spy out the land, he ascertained that it was somewhat smaller than Craik.

It was still summer of course and when they arrived the forest was abuzz with animal activity. Birdsong greeted them at the very outset, much louder than they had heard on the way, and insects were everywhere in the warm sunshine. As they entered into the forest, Badger was able to read a sign: "Welcome to Glentress Forest". He looked at his map and saw that this was indeed Glentress, and it really was a welcome moment after all the hardships of the last week. There was no time for relaxation today though. The animals had entered their new home and had to spy out the land, build a new home, find sources of food, meet new dangers that they were not yet used to, and find a school again for the kits. As Tipple was soon to experience, there was a great deal of adventure and excitement still before him.

©Courtesy of Evelyn Simak, geograph.org.uk

Map of Glentress Forest

A New Drey Begins

The squirrels thanked Badger for being their guide but Badger too was in debt for their saving his life! The creatures said their goodbyes and then they decide to split up and each family was to look for a new territory. Badger suggested that they all return here after a week to find out where the others were located. Tipple headed eastwards, Badger to the north and Forrest and Dalbeattie to the west.

Tipple, Suzy and family thus climbed the nearest fir tree and were soon on their way across the branches into a new life.
"What's for breakfast?" enquired Tim, who was ravenous.
"Let's see what we can find," replied Tipple, confident that the forest would deliver up some of its produce for them.

It was not as easy as they thought. No sooner had they spotted some luscious cones at the foot of a Norway Spruce when they were confronted by another squirrel. This was part of someone else's midden and private property. Tipple held his ground as did the other squirrel but rather than risk a fight, Tipple decided to retreat in a dignified manner. Further on, they met another red squirrel who was equally determined not to allow intruders on to his patch and he demonstratively chirped and chucked and waved his tail as a warning.

As they continued, things were a little better and the family were able to strip some bark and find a few tasty insects. After regaining some energy, they headed east past Green Hill and on towards Hope Burn. Suddenly, there was a zish at the right side of the frightened creatures, then another at the left side. Tipple scurried to the right, Suzy to the left and the others in all directions. As they looked around them the whole forest was overrun by humans on fiendish, metal contraptions. It was a Sunday and the woods were filled with mountain bikers competing in a 7Stanes bike race. Mainly on the woodland paths but also through the trees, bikers seemed to be everywhere. "This is worse than an infestation of fleas!" thought Tipple, and at the same time all the squirrels sought the safety of the branches. From there they looked down at the hullaballoo beneath them. Tipple would have happily put a few stanes in their spokes but he didn't realise that this was not an everyday occurrence. They continued further eastwards in the branches.

Soon it was time to spy out the land from the treetops. What was the forest like for a squirrel? There were plenty of Sitka and Norway Spruces, Scots pines and larches, sycamore and beech trees, ash and rowans. From the canopy, they could see the town of Peebles and where the roads were, but where were they to build a home? It seemed that the whole forest was someone else's property. After taking a look around the area, Tipple and family headed towards a place called Red Cleuch. In a large sycamore tree with plenty of cover, they stopped and listened and looked and listened again. There was plenty of birdsong, and goldcrest and blackcaps were trilling from the branches. There was no sign of a squirrel though and high up they found a nook in the trunk. Tipple stretched his neck to look inquisitively into the hole. He half expected to be confronted by another squirrel but there was no sound or movement. He climbed in, called Suzy up to inspect the hole, and sure enough it was dry and large enough for the family drey.

It was now time to gather some leaves and moss to line the nest and although the whole family was tired, they resisted the urge to take a quick nap. They had to find some food for the evening. They all took part in gathering cones for sharpening their teeth, mushrooms to hang up and dry, insects, shoots and even some old hazelnuts that another squirrel had rejected. Soon they had enough to feed the family and they scurried back to the new drey with the food supplies.

Tipple was still keen to make another summer home not too far away from the present one. There were three main reasons for this. They would not be found so easily by predators, it would be another food store and hiding place, and it would also avoid them being plagued by parasites. He wanted to avoid at all costs a late summer itching epidemic! But now the family gathered to eat and then sleep away the rest of the day and night. They were not used to such long, frantic activity and the week's journey had made them all full of aches and pains.

The next day, Tipple and Suzy were hoping to sleep a little longer than usual but they were wakened by a chomping and foot-tapping sound below them. As Tipple popped his head out of the drey, he saw another squirrel eating one of their mushrooms.
"I don't believe it!" said Tipple to himself. "Don't tell me this tree is taken as well!"
In fact it wasn't. They were just being visited by a spry, chirpy red squirrel who was curious to see who the new visitors were that had moved in.
"Good morning!" exclaimed the visitor. "My name is Frazer Squirrel and I live three trees further on."

"Is the forest so full of squirrels?" asked an exasperated Tipple.
"Yes, we're famous here, but don't worry, there's plenty of food for everybody. In fact, I wanted to share with you a few, ripe female cones from last year's harvest and from my midden," replied Frazer.
"That's very good of you," exclaimed Tipple in return. He had never experienced such hospitality before as Scottish squirrels are very careful who they give their nuts to.
Frazer Squirrel led Tipple through the trees that morning to his midden and there the two ate hungrily on a couple of pine cones and Tipple and Frazer returned to the MacRed drey with a mouthful of other cones for the others.

"Let me take you on a tour of this part of the forest," suggested the new squirrel.
The others agreed and soon they were all on their way to explore. There was still dew on the grass below and the creatures were quick to take a well-earned drink before heading further.
"You'll need to watch out for eagles around here," explained Frazer, "but they have to be good to catch the likes of us unawares."
They stopped again to descend into the undergrowth and Frazer showed them a bush of wild strawberries. They didn't need much prompting to be soon chomping on the tasty fruits. Tipple noticed other trees too that would be ripe with berries in the coming autumn.

At the eastern edge of the forest, Frazer pointed to a large building surrounded by a high fence and with a road leading probably to Peebles.
"I don't know what it is," said Frazer, "as it has been newly built and I haven't had the courage to explore it alone. There are humans there most of the day. Perhaps we can explore it together one night."
"I'm game if you are," replied Tipple in a burst of over-confidence. "I'd first like to get the children settled in though before any dangerous escapades!"
Tipple and Suzy were keen to find a school for the kits and to build a second drey. They had too to meet up with Badger and Forrest and Dalbeattie fairly soon.
"That's okay!" replied Frazer, "You just let me know when you have time."
The animals were soon back at Red Cleuch and Tipple began to look for another nest site.

Suzy meanwhile used the afternoon to meet some of the other animals and to enquire about a school. The birds were particularly informed of goings-on across the whole forest. They told her that there was a sort of learning centre for young animals at a place called West Glenbield to the north. It was run not by any bird but a very old badger and was not too difficult to reach. The birds led Suzy through the trees to the spot they had heard of, and sure enough there was a sett with a sign on it which read "Hector Badger and Sgoil". Suzy didn't know what a *sgoil* was but the chaffinches explained that Hector Badger was from the north of Scotland and this was their word for 'school'. She was quite relieved to have found the location, and with the aid of the birds and using her memory, she returned as quickly as she could to the drey.

Tipple meanwhile had found a suitable location for a second home and hideout. It was about a hundred yards from their new drey and was a sturdy ash tree. It was smitten, unfortunately, with ash die-back, a fungus infection, but this didn't seem to deter Tipple from claiming his stake. Soon it would be autumn and he would have a plentiful supply of loose twigs and leaves to build the nest.

Exactly one week after parting from his friends, Tipple returned to Cardie Hill at the entrance to the forest in the south to meet up with Badger and the two other squirrels. They had all made a new home and exchanged directions and descriptions for future visits. The biggest surprise was that Benjamin Badger had found a new activity! He had met with old Hector Badger and agreed to take over the school in the autumn. When Tipple told Suzy and the children they were overjoyed that their friend would be passing on his wise counsel.

Tipple was very pleased that night. They had a new drey that they were improving all the time, the location for a second, plenty of food supplies, they had got to know the territory a little, and they had found a new school and a new teacher for the family.

The Factory

Soon the weeks passed by and it was early autumn - a feast for squirrels. The leaves of the deciduous trees had begun to turn yellow and red, the larches were shedding their needles and the migratory birds were collecting together to fly south again after the abundance of a warm Scottish summer. Tipple felt that it was time to begin to build the second drey and whilst the kits were at school, he and Suzy were busy gathering twigs, moss, grass and leaves to place in a fork of the ash tree.

As they were gathering materials, they were met again by Frazer Squirrel. He was happy to give them a hand and soon the nest was taking shape.
"How about finding out what lies beyond the forest?" asked Frazer. "I'd love to know just what is in that building that's so carefully guarded from the outside world by the humans."
They agreed that it would be good to explore the next day, but Frazer told them that they would have to go at night when the workers were not there. The date for the foray was thus set, and the very next night with the kits tucked up warm in the drey, Tipple, Suzy and Frazer Squirrel set out to the east in search of another adventure.

As they arrived at the edge of the forest, they stopped to see what was going on at the building. There were a few trucks around but they were all silent and parked. The building itself was lit up from outside, but inside there was only the minimum of lighting. It seemed that Frazer was right - the humans were not there in the wee, small hours.

They scurried down to the ground and sped across the grassy ridge to the perimeter fencing. It was a high fence but nothing that would keep out three determined squirrels. At the top of the fence, they saw a telegraph pole and carrying on some yards at the top of the wire fence, they jumped and climbed up the wooden pole. The telephone wires veered off in two directions and they decided to take the one to the main building. Resisting the temptation to sharpen their teeth on the telecom cable, they acrobatically balanced and proceeded along the cable to the main building. There they looked around for any clues as to what might be behind the walls and windows.

Frazer had seen that one of the windows was slightly ajar, and they peered in to the semi-darkness. The air was filled with the scent of a woody, chocolatey, nutty aroma. Frazer was the first to squeeze through the window, and hanging on to a blinds cord, he lowered himself on to the floor. Tipple and

Suzy followed suit and soon all three were stood on the floor of the factory sniffing the air and trying to accustom their eyes to the twilight and shadow. They carried on towards the middle of the large hall. Frazer led the way but suddenly Suzy gave out a shriek. She had seen a large shadow approach from behind them and felt that they had been scuttled. It was only the shadow though of Frazer projected on to the wall by one of the security lights, but what a fright they all had! Regaining their composure, they approached a large, cylindrical, metal vat with a steel ladder attached to the side. Nearby, there was a conveyor belt with hundreds of jars stationed one after the other and not a single one moving! Tipple was intensely curious to find out what they contained, and jumping up he examined the containers. It was no good though - he couldn't open a single lid as they were so tightly sealed. There were a few jars with a label and scuttling over the jars without falling, he slowly began to read the labels. He was not as good as Badger at reading, but he could eventually make out what was inside.

"Joy of joys!" he cried out in raptures. "It's a Nutella factory!"
Every squirrel knew what that meant - an unending supply of hazelnut mousse! But how were they going to get the jars open? Frazer and Suzy also tried to pull open the lids on the jars and even to bite their way through, but to no avail. Tipple meanwhile, being a curious squirrel, decided to see what was in the vat. He ran up the ladders and looked down into the depths. It was full of Nutella! He balanced himself on the rim of the container and walked a good yard or two to inspect the contents. The problem was that the vat was full, but not to the brim and he couldn't reach it. He pondered over the difficulty, then decided to reach down into the mousse by rotating his rear ankles as usual. It was one thing to cling to a tree, however, and quite another thing to cling to metal. Whoosh! He lost his footing and fell head first into the paste!
"Help!" he cried remorsefully.
Suzy and Frazer darted up the ladder to see what was happening.
"Nutella!" they both cried out in unison.
"Never mind the Nutella, help me out of here!" replied Tipple.
He swam to the side and put up his paw but the other squirrels didn't want to suffer the same fate and couldn't reach him.
"Hold up your tail to us," they implored.
He did so and clutching his sticky and gooey tail, they pulled him up.

"What an indignity!" he thought to himself as he descended the ladder, licking his fur. This was a twofold experience. He enjoyed the nutty taste of the Nutella, but not the fur and hairs that stuck to his tongue. To add insult to

injury, the two others joined in the licking process and soon most of the paste
was gone.
"You'll have to have a dip in the burn before you go to bed," suggested
Frazer, "otherwise, the kits will be licking you all week!"

What a night, and worse was still to come. They decided it would be better to
leave and to come back another night with some containers for the famous
mousse. Before they got to the open window though, the nightwatchman was
doing his rounds. He had noticed small, brown footprints on the polished floor
and following them to the window he caught sight of three startled creatures,
two with Nutella-smeared mouths and one with Nutella-smeared feet.
"What on earth?!" he exclaimed in disbelief.
He disappeared and returned just as quickly as he had left waving a broom
frantically at the three animals.
"Away out of here, ye vermin! As if I have'na enough trouble wi'out a bunch of
overgrown rats!"
Hearing and seeing quite clearly that they were unwanted guests, they all
three raced up the cord of the blinds and made for the open window. Just in
time! No sooner had Suzy, as the last one of them, squeezed through the
opening, when the angry man pushed the window shut with the broom handle
and the three scampered back over the roof, the telephone lines and down
the fence back to the forest.

Once they had got their breath back, Frazer was the first to make an
observation.
"What an ungrateful lot these humans are! You'd think they would be happy to
be feeding the local wildlife, especially nut connoisseurs like us."
Tipple and Suzy were a little more pragmatic.
"I don't think we'd better try that again. These humans are too canny. They
always seem to spot us whether it's day or night," complained Tipple.
"Maybe we'd better stick to real nuts and the forest," added Suzy Squirrel.

As they returned home, tired and excited, Tipple did indeed take a wash in
the cold water of the burn. Then they said farewell to Frazer and returned to
the safety of the drey. The next day, the three kits didn't even notice that their
parents had been out on a mission of mischief, but Suzy and Tipple were
older and wiser for their adventure.

The Picnic

©Courtesy of hedera.baltica, Wikimedia Commons "Aren't I cute?!"

It was autumn. The leaves had lost their colour and a quite a few were already on the ground. It had become cooler and the berries and nuts were ripening at last. This was the time that the squirrels in the forest had been waiting for - a great feast was being prepared for them by Mother Nature and they knew that they soon had to gather and cache for the winter months.

On this particular day, Tipple was keen to be out foraging but Suzy Squirrel was decidedly unwell with a high fever. The children were at school and Tipple was alone at the drey applying various moss compressions to bring down the fever but to no avail. He knew that the deer in the forest would know of plant and herb remedies, as they were accustomed to seek out over one hundred plants in the course of a lifetime to heal various ailments. He decided it would be best to seek their advice, although he was reluctant to leave Suzy alone in the drey. Setting out over the branches, he quickly learned from the blackbirds and thrushes of the whereabouts of a party of deer. Turning west to trace these shy creatures, he found a group deep in the forest. They were slightly surprised as a voice spoke to them from above, but Tipple soon made an appearance to allay their anxiety.

"Good morning, dear deer!" exclaimed Tipple. "My wife, Suzy Squirrel, is ill in bed with a fever and I can't do anything for her. Do you know of any herbs or plants I could find in the forest?"

"Why, to be sure we do!" replied Hamish Stag, "but we don't give away our wisdom to any old animal. Who are *you* anyway? I haven't seen you in this neck of the woods before!"

"My name's Tipple MacRed Squirrel and I'm fairly new here, having lost my home in Craik Forest near to Hawick. We live over to the east of the forest but the birds told me I would find you here."

"Well come down to terra firma where I don't have to strain my neck," replied Hamish. "These antlers are quite a weight you know. I'll be glad to get rid of them this year!"

"You can give them to me if you like," replied Tipple rather cheekily. "We squirrels like nothing better than an antler or two to grind down our front teeth and to sharpen them for nut cracking."

"You're quite a forward wee chap, aren't you?" determined Hamish. •

"Just practical, just practical," said Tipple, wondering at the same time how to weasel out the information he needed from the stubborn deer.

"Well, I suppose you want to know what to give for fevers? There's a price to pay though. Haven't you heard of the saying, 'One good turn deserves another'?" replied Hamish.

Tipple thought quickly what he could give them and then he had a brainwave. All animals like food and this was just the right time to have a picnic! It may not be the best time of the year for other creatures, but it is paradise on earth for squirrels, and just what the doctor ordered for the family and Suzy.

"We are having a picnic soon," suggested Tipple, not having any idea yet of when and where. "Maybe you'd all like to come along as our guests for a feast and some conviviality?"

"Why, that's a splendid idea. I'll take you up on that." The other deer nodded in agreement. Once a deal had been settled, Hamish took Tipple to another part of the forest not too far away on foot and showed him Mother Nature's medicine chest.

"Now, laddie, this plant's just the thing for a high fever. It's called feverfew but not many animals know it can bring down a fever. Take some of the leaves with you."
Tipple gratefully plucked the green leaves and then they went a little further. "Over there is sheep sorrel. That's also good for bringing your temperature down. Then take some of the catnip over yonder. This will make your wife feel wonderfully relaxed afterwards. You squirrels also like to chew on the tree bark, don't you? Find a birch tree and chew on the bark and leaves - this will also help. Now what about this picnic?" asked Hamish impatiently.

"We live over to the east at Red Cleuch in a large sycamore tree. How about meeting there at midday the day after tomorrow? We'll of course provide the food!" said Tipple.
The deer all agreed that this was a good idea and then Tipple ran up the nearest tree to regain his orientation, and clutching his collection of leaves from the various plants, he sprang from tree to tree to return to the drey.
He immediately gave Suzy Squirrel some of the feverfew to chew on but she found it very bitter. Ever resourceful, Tipple Squirrel had been able to pick some birch bark on the way as Hamish had suggested and he gave her this as well along with some catnip. Soon Suzy was fast asleep, and Tipple was able to ponder on how to feed a group of deer in two days' time. What on earth do deer eat, he thought to himself?

The next day Suzy had completely recovered as Hamish Stag had said she would, and the two squirrels were able to leave the drey in search of goodies for the picnic. The day was warm and sunny and the forest was alive with the sound of various creatures looking for food or simply enjoying the peace and the warm sunshine. It wasn't long before Suzy spotted a walnut tree and they scampered down to pick a few, ripe fruits. Then it was on to a rosehip bush and then a Virginia creeper for some berries. Each time, they returned to the drey armed to the teeth with walnuts and berries. After that, they found a rowan tree and picked the red berries, then some blueberries and finally some crab apples. Tipple felt that there weren't enough nuts, so they ventured out again to find some acorns from an old oak tree. These too they painstakingly brought back to the drey. Tipple wished he were a kangaroo and had a large pocket to carry things in.
"How are we going to carry all this with us on the picnic?" enquired Tipple of Suzy, "And what on earth are we to collect for the deer?"

They both decided that they needed a bag of some kind to carry everything and this time they set out to find where humans had been. Soon they were at a clearing in the forest with benches, tables and a refuse bin. Tipple popped into the bin and scrambling through the papers and plastic, he came across a plastic bag. He placed it on the floor and opening it with his teeth and paws, he clambered inside to inspect it. It was indeed dry and clean and just the thing for the picnic. Suzy joined him in holding one edge of the bag and as they climbed back up the fir trees they looked as if they were carrying a sail or paraglider.

Suzy had seen that deer eat bark too, and roots and leaves, and they set about collecting these in the plastic bag along with shoots and grass as they busily hopped from tree to ground. Tipple also spotted some yarrow which he knew was good for inhibiting the spread of parasites in the nest, and this went into the bag as well. Soon it was fit to burst, and they hauled the food package all the way back to the drey. The birds were astonished to see what they were doing and wondered where they could find a similar bag to increase their food stock. Back at the drey, they decided that the best place for the picnic would be a sunny spot near to Hope Burn where all could also have a cool, refreshing drink. This would not be in the open as the deer would be too nervous about predators and they couldn't disappear up a tree so easily as a squirrel.

The next day all was ready, and around midday, the group of deer headed by Hamish Stag arrived in good time at the foot of the sycamore tree. They weren't sure though if this was the right location. Sure enough though, Tipple appeared from behind the trunk as if someone had just pressed a switch and greeted the animal friends.
"Good day, dear deer!" he spluttered out, always ready to tease his fellow creatures.
"Good day to you, Tipple MacRed Squirrel. I hope you're bright-eyed and bushy-tailed," he responded jokingly.

Tipple was soon joined by the rest of the family and they explained where they were to hold the picnic. The animals set off, the youngsters all holding the large plastic bag above their heads. Tipple had also planned ahead that morning and he and Suzy had already taken some berries and nuts and bark to the picnic location. Suzy had remained there on guard so that they didn't disappear into the hungry mouths of birds or other squirrels, and they soon all met up at the burn.

Tipple and Suzy were keen to find out about how the deer live and what dangers they face and avoid, and soon Hamish and the others were deep in conversation, whilst the kits and fawns munched away to their heart's content and then left the others to play.

"How did you get such knowledge about medicinal plants?" asked a curious Tipple.

"It's been passed down to us from generation to generation. Other animals know instinctively which plants to use when sick but nobody knows as many as we do," replied Hamish proudly.

"Do tell us about how you live and how you avoid dangers," added Suzy.

"Well, we're forest creatures too you know, and only venture out into the open when there's a shortage of food in the woods and there are no dangers. We eat practically everything but prefer mushrooms, fruit, berries, nuts and shoots. Oh, yes and tree bark too - very tasty! There are no big predators like bears or wolves anymore, but the biggest predators are humans. They like to hunt us more than anything else, and eat us too if they get the chance. We can run very fast though - up to 40 mph when there are no trees in the way."

"I expect you have good vision with all your hind-sight!" suggested Tipple cheekily.

Hamish was not amused and continued to chew nonchalantly.

"This time of year is a highlight for me," said Hamish after a slight pause. "We have a sort of stag party with other male deer called the 'rut' when we fight with each other with our long antlers for access to the females - and don't you dare say, Tipple Squirrel, that you expect we get into a rut now and again! After a few fights and posturing a little, we mate with the females and then our antlers drop off."

Tipple couldn't help laughing as he brought the one occurrence with the other in association.

"Just you behave yourself in front of our guests," interrupted a cross Suzy Squirrel with a look of consternation.

After a hearty meal, the animals walked over to the burn and enjoyed a nice cool, refreshing drink of the crystal-clear water, engaged once again in conversation, and then bade farewell to each other, intending to maintain their friendship with each other come what may.

On the way back over the trees, Tipple and Suzy heard from the birds that there were humans with cameras on the forest paths. The word was out amongst the tree-dwelling creatures not to show themselves, but to sing loudly in hiding, as this infuriates people. Tipple though was curious as ever and didn't want to miss the opportunity of a photo shoot. Learning where the humans were to be found, he sprang across the trees in a westerly direction. There were indeed three people below with cameras and long lenses.

"Just my chance!" thought Tipple to himself, and adjusting his ear tufts and brushing his tail, he descended to the floor at the edge of the forest. There he pretended to be burying some nuts.
"Oh look! A cute little squirrel!" one of the human party cried out.
This was Tipple's cue. Holding a freshly plucked acorn to look even cuter, and pulling in his waistline, he grinned at the camera lenses that were directed his way. Then, after he was certain that he had been captured on film for all eternity, he scampered back up a tree, wagged his tail as if to say farewell, and then rejoined the family back at the drey.

What a day it had been and it wasn't over yet, but now all the family were quite tired and eager to take a rest in the comfort and security of the drey. Tipple thought about all the work still to do - caching nuts, collecting pine cones for the midden, and of course building a second drey for the next summer. Despite all this, it was a happy and contented Tipple Squirrel that snuggled up to Suzy that evening.

The Hunting Party

Tipple was busy collecting acorns and other nuts for caching as well as picking some left-over blueberries he had found. He was quite mathematical in his choice of a cache location and each nut was carefully inspected and then buried in a zig-zag line exactly one yard apart to avoid finders-keepers.

Suddenly, there was a loud crash nearby in the forest. It sounded like gunfire, and Tipple ran up a nearby spruce tree to see what it was. Another two shots rang out and there were humans shouting loudly and animals and birds taking to flight. Carefully concealing himself as best he could in the evergreens, he approached the scene of the danger. There were five or six men down below all with guns and three dogs. Hunters! This was the start of the hunting season right enough, but normally not a problem for a squirrel. Then a shot ricocheted behind him, and then another and another.
"They're after me too," said Tipple and he hid behind the trunk.
This was no photo shoot but real, deadly shooting and Tipple was in the line of fire. He attempted to get back on to a branch and to leave the scene but to no avail as yet another shot whistled by. These were no ordinary hunters but poachers, and very much of the 'kill it and grill it' variety. What could Tipple do to avert their attention?

Just as he was thinking of throwing something down at the group, they were called over in the other direction. There were deer, and they let off two salvoes. Two of the deer fell to the ground, and they were followed up by the dogs barking loudly. The men all rushed over to the prey, giving Tipple chance to climb higher and to find a hiding place in the nook of a fir tree. After recovering his breath, he ventured to take a look at what was going on. With his exceptional focusing ability, he could see that two deer were dead and covered in blood but that the others had managed to escape. There was one stag and one doe but Tipple ascertained that it wasn't his friend Hamish that had been felled. The men pulled back the dogs and tied up the feet of the two dead animals. A large SUV arrived, and the carcasses were thrown into the back of the vehicle. Slamming the door shut, they were still intent on finding more prey. Two of the hunters shot up into the trees once again, this time at a pair of blackbirds but they missed. Then a jay was their target and this time it was a hit, the poor bird falling softly to the forest floor.
"Why are they shooting at birds and squirrels?" asked Tipple to himself and soon there was another frightened animal in their sights. It was a wild hare and this too had no chance against the powerful calibres and telescopic

sights. It was pounced on by one of the dogs and picked up in its mouth, shaken wildly, and then brought back to its master.

Tipple was aghast that his friends had been killed and that he had not been able to do anything about it, but he was still too scared to move from his hiding place with the hunters down below. The hunting party continued to scour the forest for anything alive that they could find. It was clear that they were not just after meat to sell but also out for shooting practice under the motto 'the only good forest is a dead forest'. Indeed, the slaughter went on for over an hour, and Tipple could see that they had bagged not only the deer and hare but many birds, two young fawns, and a couple of weasels. Then they all returned to the SUV as if they were aware that their time unnoticed by the authorities was limited, and clambered into the vehicle. They then sped off towards the south of the forest and the main road.

Tipple crawled out of his nook and after waiting a minute to see that all was clear again, he was in two minds as to what to do. Should he return to the drey to break the awful news to the others or should he pay his respects to his dead friends? He decided on the latter and clambered down the trunk of the fir tree over to the scene where the deer had been shot. The forest was deathly silent. All the birds and animals had left the location and Tipple felt utterly alone. The ground where the deer had lain was flattened still by their weight and there were pools of fresh blood leading away to tyre tracks from the SUV. He thought for a moment of the picnic only a few weeks earlier and how fragile life is, then he decided he could do no more and jumped up one of the trees out of danger again.

As he made his way through the forest, he had forgotten all about caching and the midden and even the second drey. The forest was not the same again and he made his way back home to tell the others of the sad news and how he himself had nearly been shot. Suzy and the kits had also heard the shots and that the animals were not at ease, but they weren't sure why, and Suzy had called the kits back from playing into the safety of the drey.

"There's been a terrible shooting," explained Tipple. "Many animals and birds have been killed by poachers and two of the deer from the picnic have been slain."
They were all very upset and decided to stay home for the rest of the day. As if the weather was also commiserating with the dead animals and the feelings of their fellow creatures, it began to rain heavily shortly after Tipple had returned. He did not eat that evening and went to bed being thankful that he

was still alive and there for the family, but somewhat thoughtful and remorseful as his tired eyes closed, and he drifted off into a refreshing sleep.

Fire!

It was late autumn now and work on the second drey or summer nest was coming along nicely. Tipple had found a suitable tree - an ash - and he had built the structure from various twigs, moss and bark. He had lined the inside with bracken and moss and was now applying the finishing touches to the second home. He was keen too to make some "beds" again for the children and was on the lookout for some suitable materials.

The migratory birds had long since left the forest and flown south for warmer climes, but there was still plenty of birdsong from thrushes and coal tits, blackbirds and ever-loyal crossbills. All the other red squirrels were also busy collecting food for the winter months and Tipple and Suzy had been visited recently not only by Frazer Squirrel but also Forrest and Dalbeattie Squirrel from the north of the forest where they had successfully settled. The children were catered for at school by old Benjamin Badger who had taken over from the even older Hector, and they were all progressing in practical skills and wisdom needed to survive and thrive.

One day, Tipple and Suzy were out collecting pines from the uppermost branches of the fir trees when the sky became very dark. The birds too had noticed the change in the weather and a strong westerly wind began to blow. The female cones at the very tips of the utmost branches were the most tasty but now it was becoming more difficult to balance as the branches swayed about in the wind.

Tipple actually enjoyed testing out his coordination and balancing skills and was keen to add to the middens near to the drey. Suddenly, there was a flash of lightning that swept across the sky and lit up the dark clouds, followed by heavy thunder a few seconds later. It was time to take cover. The last thing Tipple and Suzy wanted was a singed tail! They scampered back to the drey across the treetops. Before they could reach home, there was another flash of lightning and then another, followed by peals of thunder but no rain. As they reached the drey, Tipple could see a flock of rooks and crows leaving the forest and heading west. There was smoke too as if someone had started a fire down below. Soon the news began to spread across the treetops that an old diseased ash tree had been hit by lightning and was burning. This was a real worry as the trees in the forest were so close together and there had not been any rain for some weeks. This meant that the bare trees and brown bracken were all dry and flammable.

Soon the smoke had grown from a single column to a large, black cloud and the forest animals were starting to run in panic across the floor of the woods. It was a forest fire and the wind was spreading it in the direction of Tipple and Suzy. There was nothing for it but to collect the kits from school and to move westwards. Hares, rabbits and other small mammals were darting below them as they left the drey and many birds had taken to the skies.

Once they had collected the children and left them in the care of Benjamin Badger who had cancelled the school on hearing the news, they returned to save their homes and to see how far and how fast the fire had spread. Fanned by the wind and fuelled by the dryness of the vegetation, the fire was covering ground rapidly like an advancing wave. The humans too had seen that the forest was aflame and there was the sound of sirens and fire engines coming from Peebles and Innerleithen.

Returning to the main drey, Tipple and Suzy collected the plastic bag that they had used for the picnic foods and headed to the main midden. The caches would be alright as the nuts were all buried under the soil, but the two squirrels were aware that their pine cones had to be saved from the advancing flames or they would be faced with hunger in the winter. They scampered down to the main midden and picked up the cones with paws and teeth and placed them quickly in to the plastic bag. There were more than they could carry but they shared the weight and carried the burden between them. The smoke was everywhere and as well as having difficulty breathing, their eyes were sore too. Indeed, before the flames came even nearer, they decided to leave as quickly as possible.

From a safe distance, Tipple and Suzy observed that tree after tree was being consumed. All the birds and animals had left but the vegetation was disappearing fast. They watched silently as the flames reached the ash tree where Tipple had built the summer home. There was nothing they could do but watch passively as the nest was eaten up by the flames.
"All that hard work!" sighed Tipple and resigned himself to the fact that a third home had been lost, this time to nature's whim. Still, the family was safe, and they headed back to the main drey to deposit the cones.

From there they could see that there were many humans battling the fire with water and wooden brooms and that they were trying to create a natural barrier to stop the spread westwards. Soon the squirrels were joined by Badger and the kits who wanted to make sure that their parents were also safe. By late afternoon, it seemed that the fire was under control and that the drey, the sycamore tree and the other trees round about were saved. There was a great sigh of relief from the MacReds one and all and Badger too. His sett to the north could also have been in danger if the fire had got out of control.

The animals decided to celebrate with some cones and for Badger some dried mushrooms from the larder that Suzy Squirrel had been saving for a special occasion. This was indeed a special occasion.
"There's nothing like a warm fire in the autumn and winter to keep the blood strong!" added Badger wryly. The six creatures had once again survived to enjoy another day.

Cousins from America

One day as Tipple was busy stocking up his midden and caching beech nuts and white acorns for the coming winter, he was distracted by the calling of Suzy Squirrel back at the drey. It wasn't a call of alarm but one of excitement and Tipple wondered what to expect as he finished tidying up the midden.

Back at the drey there was wild excitement and strange voices. The first he recognized - they were being visited by Forrest and Dalbeattie Squirrel which was always welcome - but there were strangers too. He scurried up to the drey and there indeed were Suzy and Forrest and Dalbeattie with two small striped squirrels.
"Tipple, we would like you to meet some cousins from America who have flown over all the way from Colorado in the western United States. This is Chuck and Rusty Chipmunk," explained Forrest.
"Hi, buddie!" said Rusty.
"Hi Tip!" said Chuck.

Chuck and Rusty from Colorado

A cold shiver went down Tipple's spine. One thing he hated more than anything was being called "Tip"!
"Good day to you," replied Tipple trying to be at his polite best as Suzy Squirrel scowled at him.

"Wow, dig that red fur coat and those ear tufts! You Scottish squirrels really are so cute!" replied Chuck looking him over from head to foot, "And that bushy tail. What a specimen, dude!"
Tipple squeamed in embarrassment at the same time thinking it would have been good to have one of Badger's dictionaries to hand.
"So this is a drey," said Rusty Chipmunk. "Ain't it just cute, but so passé. How do you guys live in such discomfort with a family of five? A grizzly would be up here before you could say John Deere!"
Tipple looked in consternation first at Forrest and then at Suzy and decided he needed an interpreter.
"What's a grizzly?" he asked.
"Why it's the biggest animal on the planet and fierce, my is it fierce, and can chew you up in a few seconds! Have you guys never seen a grizzly bear?" asked Chuck with surprise.
"No, I ain't," replied Tipple sarcastically and was hit on the back by Suzy.
"This drey stuff is just so antiquated. We're mainly ground squirrels and live in the ground in burrows. The tunnels are up to 3.5 metres long and we have escape routes all over. One of our neighbours is always on the watch too for grizzlies or coyots," continued Chuck.
"What's a coyote?" asked Tipple once again.
"Why I don't know either," replied Chuck. "We have coyots. They're the biggest predator on the prairies and will swallow you whole if you give them the chance!"

Tipple decided that he would show them his artisanal skills inside the drey. First the dining area, then the large larder where he had a stock of dried mushrooms and fresh acorns.
"It's just like we imagined it would be - real olde worlde. Very nice, but you guys really are in the dark ages!" added Rusty.
"You don't happen to have some brownies, do you?" asked Chuck, feeling a little peckish.
Tipple looked around in consternation. The only brownies he knew were part of the girl guides back in Hawick. What would he be doing with brownies? Forrest explained that it was a type of cake in America.
"Oh, we call them buns or biscuits in this country. Hasn't changed since the dark ages," mused Tipple.

Then Tipple showed them the sycamore tree and some silver birches and elms and then a Scots pine and a Sitka spruce. The chipmunks were delighted to see such a variety in the forest which meant a plentiful supply of food.

"Back in Colorado we have the biggest trees in the world - sequoias - my, are they good to climb, and aspen, Ponderosa pines and junipers."
Tipple didn't know these but he was interested to find out more. He then took them down to his cache area and the main midden with its pile of ripe cones.
"How do you stop the other animals from eating them all?" asked Rusty.
"One of us has to stand guard over them and mark them with our scent glands," explained Tipple to the guests.
Rusty and Chuck were simply overwhelmed. "What a lot of drudgery! Back in the States, we have iMiddens! That stands for intelligent middens and they are attached directly to the burrows in various larders so we don't have to guard anything. Every midden has a window and we keep a check on the stocks every day using the windows so that we know exactly what's where, and we are never without food. Other chipmunks or rock squirrels or woodchucks have no chance to get at our larders. Before each larder is a line of twigs and wood chippings which we can light at any time there's danger. We call this a firewall - total security in our high-tech burrows." explained Rusty.

Tipple was mighty impressed, but in Scotland tradition had always proved reliable and he didn't fancy living in the ground like a mole or a vole.
"How did you chipmunks get to Scotland? asked Tipple with some curiosity. "Surely you're not flying squirrels as well?"
"Well we certainly flew - third class in fact and very comfy too!"
Rusty explained that they had smuggled their way to Denver Airport on a truck, and then before the plane to Edinburgh was loaded with the baggage, they had run across the tarmac, up the hold gangway and into the baggage compartment. No-one had seen them and avoiding the flying cases as best they could, they snuggled up on a case near a window for the duration of the flight. When they arrived, they did the same in reverse, finding a truck heading south and voilà - they were in Peebles and then Glentress Forest to visit their cousins Forrest and Dalbeattie.

Tipple was amazed at their audacity and ingenuity and said he would like one day to see America for himself. After the tour, the animals had a meal of berries and insects for starters, then a main course of pine cones and acorns, then a vintage sap and some rose hip syrup. After the meal, the chipmunks introduced the red squirrels to a game of Chinese whispers which even the kits joined in with and they all had a great deal of fun.

As it was becoming late, the MacReds bade farewell to Forrest and Dalbeattie and to their guests from America, saying they would meet up again soon.

"Quite a handful, these foreigners, with all their 'we have the biggest and the best' conversations," said Tipple to Suzy.

"I think they're really cute," replied Suzy, "and very brisk and lively. They're here for a few weeks I heard and will certainly brighten up the winter this year."

"I think we ought to show them how we live here and enjoy it too," added Tipple. "I'd like to organise a ceilidh soon with all our forest friends so that we can show them some good, old-fashioned Scottish hospitality."

"What a good idea," said Suzy, and as they retired for the night they were thinking of how to arrange things.

A Ceilidh

The first cold days of winter were once again descending on the forest which was transcended by an eerie calm from the treetops. All the song birds had left for Africa and the animals had been busy in the autumn gathering supplies. Tipple was now engaged in the rebuilding of his summer home and was looking for suitable materials - lichen, moss, etc.

As he was working, he remembered how successful the wedding had been in the forest clearing back at Craik and he thought it would be a good idea to invite as many animals as possible to the ceilidh - the deer, Forrest and Dalbeattie Squirrel, Frazer Squirrel, Benjamin Badger, hares, rabbits, weasels and owls (that could be trusted), and of course the birds. They would meet at the centre of the forest so that no-one would have so far to travel and it would be held in the evening after dark for safety. This time all the animals would be responsible for providing food and drink and the owls and the woodpeckers and other birds would provide the music. The kits had also learned at school how to mimic the very mainstay of Scottish musical culture - the bagpipes! It would be a fun night.

All the animals met one night in November at Stotfield Knowe in the heart of the forest and the woods were a hub of activity. They had all brought something to eat which nature provided in abundance at this time of the year and there were pools of water to drink from. The chipmunks were there too of course and were thrilled to meet so many different animals. A deer and two birds were posted as lookouts for any dangers as the deer were particularly nervous, and then the feast began.

Tipple was keen to pull the American cousins' leg and asked politely, "Can I offer you a bap?" Of course neither Chuck nor Rusty knew what this was and it was certain that Tipple didn't have one either. Instead he offered them some beech nuts and acorns which they gladly added to their own supplies of berries, seeds, insects and worms. Tipple and Suzy were offered a worm each but politely refused. Rusty was very keen to tell his friends about life in Colorado, how huge the forests are and how they like to tease the raccoons. "Then there are the ranches, the Rocky Mountains and the town of Severance which is close to where we live. Buddy, you can eat alfalfa there till it's coming out of your ears! Of course you have to catch it before the farmer sprays it with all sorts of pesticides. And the snow in winter - it can truly bury you."

Tipple was very curious about all these new experiences though he had to ask what alfalfa was. After eating and drinking and blether and a good deal of teasing of their American guests and their funny accents, it was on to the main event of the night - the dancing and music. The woodpeckers provided the beat, the birds the Scottish melodies, and the kits the sounds of bagpipes! The chipmunks had never heard such sound and were soon to be overwhelmed with the fast and furious dancing provided by the animals. There were the Gay Gordons, reels and jigs, strathspeys and a dance called the Frisky performed by the squirrels with Benjamin Badger as the dance caller:
"Gie yoursels a guid shoogle (shake). That's it, then
pit your hauns on your hurdies (hips).
Baith airms in the air. Touch your heid, shooders, taes.
Gie your bahookie (bottom) a guid skelp (slap)."

Then the squirrels placed some branches on the floor in a cross shape and the other animals - apart from the deer who were considered too big - danced a sort of sword dance.

When everyone was out of breath, they went back to eating and drinking the goodies to keep up their energy levels. Badger was then called upon to tell a story and everyone was engrossed to hear the tale of the puddock (frog) and the bubblyjock (turkey). Chuck and Rusty had never had so much fun and the feasting went long into the wee, small hours. With no interruption from humans, who were all hopefully tucked up in bed, and no predators on the prowl, the ceilidh finally came to a close and the animals retired to their different locations in the forest with the idea of another ceilidh sometime soon.

The whole area where the event had taken place was covered with the remains of food and all the vegetation was beaten down by the dancing and feasting. A human coming upon the scene would have wondered what had been happening, but soon the forest was engulfed in an eerie silence once again till the dawn chorus would bring the animals back to life.

In the course of the next few weeks, Tipple and Suzy saw quite a lot of their chipmunk cousins. They took them on a tour of the forest, a visit to the Nutella factory (though they didn't venture in this time, and Chuck and Rusty told Tipple that this was Hazelnut Cream in Colorado), showed them their main haunts and hiding places, and of course the animals' school. In fact, Tipple, after his initial reluctance, had grown quite fond of the little critters and as their time to depart drew near he was keen to find a suitable going-away present for them. As he was a capable wood craftsman, he decided to create a wooden sculpture of himself. Using his paws to grip the wood and gnawing away at the piece of soft pine wood, he was able to complete a statue some five inches in height complete with tufts, bulging eyes and bushy tail within a couple of weeks. He then dyed the wood with berry juice so that it was a red squirrel and put it to dry in the larder of the drey.

Soon it was time for the chipmunks to make their way home to America and the MacRed family, Forrest and Dalbeattie Squirrel and Benjamin Badger gathered together to wish their cousins farewell. It had been an exciting time for the forest and the squirrels had been well and truly informed and entertained. Then it was Tipple's turn to say goodbye. Clutching the statue behind his back, he then presented the astonished chipmunks with their present.
"Why, who is this?" asked Chuck in surprise.
"It's an iMac," replied Tipple with pride. "The i stands for irrepressible."
Indeed, that was exactly what it was - an irrepressible Tipple MacRed Squirrel.

A New Settlement and Highway Arrives

It was now cold and dark but winter had not yet fully arrived at Glentress. In late December the trees were visited with the first hoar frosts and then came the snow which was just what Tipple had been waiting for. Why would a squirrel look forward to a snowfall? Well, Tipple and Suzy were unusual squirrels and very particular about their hygiene, and especially the parasites that come every summer and make their homes in their fur. As well as nit picking and placing yarrow in the nests, the squirrel family would take a good, long grass bath in the summer, a good, long sand bath in the autumn and you guessed it - a snow bath in the winter to remove as many parasites as possible.

As soon as the ground was covered with a carpet of snow, Tipple and Suzy rolled around in the cold, white element. Tipple would rub his face and head in the snow too and then tend to the arms, under the arms, all the cheeky bits and then between the toes. The whole process was a sort of reverse sauna for squirrels. Then it was the turn of the kits but as usual they were nowhere to be found. They hated these rituals and were in hiding!
"Okay, let's have you!" shouted an enthusiastic Tipple, but there was not a single sound to be heard.
"If you rascals don't come here at once there will be no food for you for a whole week!"
For the kits, being without food was like sleeping upright. After a few minutes, reluctant steps could be heard from the whitened-over bushes and the three kits appeared with the glummest of faces.
"Must we bathe in the snow? It's so cold and wet!" cried Jenny.
"Yes, you must!" replied Tipple determinedly.

Soon the three were bathing too in the snow and pretending to chatter their teeth to demonstrate their reluctance to their father. Suzy and Tipple supervised the proceedings and then dried off the kits with some fallen autumn leaves and bracken. Now the whole family was squeaky clean in every sense of the word!

It wasn't long before the snow became a regular occurrence, and the shortened days and increasing cold led to a change in the squirrels' metabolism with a lot more sleeping during the day. They made their main forays early in the morning and a couple of hours before sundown. Tipple and

Suzy had experienced their autumn moult. Now their fur was darker, longer and more resistant to the cold. Tipple's tufts were also longer at this time of the year.

It was during one of his forays that Tipple was once again to experience both misfortune and tragedy. He was at the eastern periphery of the forest near to the Nutella factory when there was the rumble of trucks and four-wheel drive vehicles. The lumberjacks were back! What were they going to do this time? Day after day, Tipple looked on as tree after tree was felled at the outer reaches of his territory. What were the humans up to this time? Soon he decided to bring Frazer Squirrel, who lived nearby, along to try and ascertain what was happening. He couldn't work out what the men were up to either and they looked on in dismay as their habitat was diminished, tree for tree.

After the forest had been well and truly fragmented at its eastern edge, there was a pause of a few days, then another rumble of traffic as trucks and bulldozers and mechanical diggers made their way to where the trees had once stood. It was a large area, still covered with grass, bracken, flowers and tree stumps but soon there was a commotion as the heavy machinery started to dig up the stumps, and large oblong holes were dug into the terrain. After a couple of weeks of digging, various trenches were excavated and strange poles with wires jutting out of the tops were inserted into the ground. Tipple had never seen anything like this before and he thought it was time to visit Benjamin Badger in the north of the forest for his advice.

Tipple arrived there one afternoon and found Badger busy with his books preparing for the next day of schooling. He explained to Badger in detail what he had seen and then Badger consulted one of his maps of the forest.
"It seems to me as if the humans are going to build houses from what you've described - and not just a few. Where there are houses there are also shops and factories and roads. It doesn't sound very good to me," explained Badger remorsefully.

Once the digging had finished, the trucks with earth and the construction machinery moved off and for the rest of the winter there was a pause and the animals could enjoy the tranquillity of the forest once more. Once the spring weather arrived though there was another invasion of trucks, machines and humans with funny, yellow helmets. The construction work was on in earnest. First the many houses were built all very close together with hardly space for a territory thought Tipple. Then work began on expanding the industrial estate and once again many trees, mostly conifers, were felled to make way for enterprise.

"Why do the humans have to build new homes?" thought Tipple. "We make do with existing places in trees and just improve them."
By the onset of summer, Tipple and his family had got used to the daytime disturbance of machinery, hammers, chain saws, saws of all types, and heavy diggers. The humans had also started to build a main road and this was completed very quickly for the construction teams to reach the sites as quickly and easily as possible.

By the autumn, there was a new settlement and the road was as busy as the one to Peebles. It was only a stone's throw from the houses to the summer nest and another stone's throw to the MacRed drey. Soon there were not just a few humans coming into the forest but a horde - and all with dogs - which made life very difficult for the squirrels to reach their cones and nuts without being chased. The tranquillity of the forest had been broken too and the bright lights from the streets illuminated the night sky like an orange sphere. The birds had got used to the new environment and some were taking advantage of the crumbs and refuse left by the humans, but for a bright, red squirrel it was too dangerous to venture down to the forest floor. All the other animals had also moved into the interior of the forest.

One day, Tipple and Suzy were visited by an out of breath Frazer Squirrel.
"Tipple, Suzy, come quickly! Something terrible has happened."
The two squirrels ran to accompany Frazer as they headed in the direction of the new road. Then they were distraught. A young squirrel had been run over by a vehicle and was lying motionless in the middle of the highway.
"I think it's Tim," said Frazer disconsolately.

The three squirrels ran to the side of the busy road and were oblivious to the heavy traffic. They were overcome with the noise of passing vehicles and the rush of wind deafened them. Nevertheless, Tipple and Suzy with heavy hearts could see that it was Tim Squirrel. He was not moving and lying in a small pool of blood.
"I must go and rescue him," said Tipple and attempted to find a gap in the traffic.
"That's suicide!" shouted Frazer Squirrel. "He's probably dead and you can't do anything more for him. You'll kill yourself too if you set foot on the road."
Tipple was not going to leave his eldest son though if he was still alive and he tried desperately to dodge the traffic in a zig-zag movement which he hoped would confuse the humans. He reached the site where Tim was lying and pushed desperately at his son but it was to no avail. He was already dead. Tipple tried to pick him up to take him back to the forest.
"Look out, Tipple!" shouted his friend Frazer.

Tipple turned his head to the left and saw a giant truck heading towards him. There was no way of escape and the driver was not going to brake. Tipple closed his eyes to await his death but the vehicle passed over his head and he found himself between the wheels of the juggernaut. Soon he appeared again at the other end and Suzy and Frazer shouted at him.
"Come on, Tipple! Run back to the side of the road!"
Tipple did as he was told this time in a sort of dazed trance and was once again in safety. The three squirrels headed for the forest as quickly as possible and were soon scampering over the branches of the fir trees back to the MacRed drey.

Tim Squirrel had become an unknown victim and statistic of human roadkill. Frazer stayed for a while with the stricken pair and then made his way sadly back to his own drey. Tipple's eldest son's life had been destroyed. How do squirrels mourn the loss of a loved one? They stayed in the drey for many days, not venturing out even to collect food and it was a long time before they regained their zap and energy. Life had to go on though, and the next problem for Tipple and Suzy was what to do about the new settlement and its many dangers?

Part Three

The Stowaways - Part One

By the time that the family had overcome their grief, it was once again the onset of spring and the forest was beginning to come alive to the sound of insects and songbirds. Buds were beginning to appear on the deciduous trees and flowers were beginning to grow again. New vigour was also pumped into the lifeblood of our squirrel family.

Tipple had decided to look for another drey closer to the centre of the forest but this was not so easy. Finding a drey was not a big problem but finding a new, undisturbed territory was another. Each time he carried out a scouting mission he was sent fleeing by another red squirrel defending its patch in the crowded woods, or he was disturbed by the recreational activity of humans driving, walking, jogging or mountain biking their way along the many forest trails. He didn't know the area too well either and had to be particularly careful at this time of year for pine martens and birds of prey. Tipple decided it was time to confer once again with his long-time friend Benjamin Badger.

Badger was not at home when Tipple arrived but he soon returned after collecting food for his sett larder.
"Good afternoon, Tipple," he called out to his rodent friend. "You look very troubled. What's playing on your mind?"
Tipple told Badger the news of his son's death on the road and the infringements on his territory from the new settlement. He recounted too the difficulty in finding a new territory in this crowded part of the forest.
"I thought the humans would cause you trouble. They're expanding their activities all the time and they're very unpredictable. Let's take a look at my maps of the forest."

The two creatures entered the safety of the sett where Badger lit a candle or two he had found. They carefully observed the lie of the land although Badger was much more proficient at comprehending the human signs and symbols.
"What do you need for a new territory?" asked Badger.
"A tree of my own," explained Tipple. "Then a hole in the tree for a drey and a place to create a midden. There has to be a plentiful supply of food, hiding places, no other squirrels in the vicinity and peace and quiet."
"That's a tall order," explained the badger. "This forest is so over-populated and used so often for recreation by the humans. Maybe you should consider another move."

"Another move?" asked Tipple. "I haven't got over the first one yet and what about the schooling for the kits?"
He then thought of explaining to Suzy Squirrel about another move and then he had a headache again.
"Cheer up!" said Badger. "Let's take a look at the surrounding area."

Badger looked carefully at the map. The next big forest was Castle O'er to the south.
"I've heard that there's a lot of space there for animals and it's only about 30 miles from here," explained Badger.
"Thirty miles!" cried Tipple. "How am I going to explain to Suzy Squirrel that we have to move 30 miles? I won't be allowed to set foot in the drey for a week!"
"Well, it's only about the same distance that we marched from Craik to Glentress. I know you'll be on your own this time, Tipple, but it's direct south from here - you can't miss it!" added Badger.
"I can't even find my buried nuts sometimes, never mind a forest," replied Tipple disconsolately, "but we'll manage somehow. I shall miss you all of course but I want to find somewhere where the kits can grow up and thrive in peace."
"I understand, Tipple. Have you never thought of making a burrow?! You know you're safer there than in a tree," postulated Badger.

Tipple was not convinced, and as he said farewell to his friend, he thought about getting food together for the journey and explaining to the family that they were going to move again. The next day, Tipple set about gathering some food which included roots, buds, bark, cones and even some crisps left on a trail by the humans. He carefully brought these back to the drey over a period of three days so as not to arouse suspicions and placed them in the larder. Then it was time to break the news.

"We're going on a trip," said Tipple hesitantly. The children were overjoyed.
"Where to? Where to?" they cried.
"Er, to a forest called Castle O'er," replied Tipple encouraged by his children's enthusiasm.
"A forest?" asked Suzy Squirrel. "Are we visiting someone?"
"Well, not exactly. I thought it would be a good idea to find a new home away from the memory of Tim's death and far from the interference of humans," explained Tipple.
"So that's why you've been busy filling our larder with food," stated Suzy.
"And where exactly is this forest? Is there a school and a drey and plenty of food and what about our drey here and our caches?"

"It's to the south, about thirty miles, and I don't know yet if there's a school or not," replied Tipple.

"Thirty miles and no school! Have you gone nuts, Tipple Squirrel?" cried Suzy in disbelief. "We don't know what's there, and who's going with us?"

"We'll be on our own this time," replied Tipple, "but let's think about it overnight and we can talk about it again in the morning."

This idea was the best that her husband had had thought Suzy as they retired for the night.

It wasn't long though before events were to take a turn that would change all their plans. The very next morning as they were all at breakfast and still without a thought of whether they would leave or not, there was a terrible shock awaiting them.

The drey began to shudder and swing. Outside there was the noise of a chain saw and a group of tree fellers with a large lorry. They were from the Forestry Commission and were collecting trees for a sawmill and Tipple's sycamore tree was on the list! Tipple looked out in consternation from the drey and realised that there was not much time left before the tree was felled.

"We're not leaving our drey this time," said Tipple defiantly, "This is my tree!"

The four squirrels hung on to whatever they could hold on to in the drey, including one another, and soon the tree was falling heavily to the ground.

"Jump into the sleeping area!" cried Tipple. "It will cushion the fall."

This they did and managed to escape any injuries. The fall was also cushioned by the tree's branches which caught on the other trees. Then Tipple looked out again to see what was happening on the forest floor. A group of men approached the sycamore tree and started to saw off the branches, and then a huge machine arrived, at which point Tipple and Suzy retired to the very back of the drey. It was a crane and very soon the trunk and the defiant squirrels were being picked up from the forest floor and loaded on to the truck with a number of other trees. Three chains were thrown over the load and noisily secured, and Tipple heard that the truck was heading to a sawmill near Newton Stewart, wherever that was. They would have to leave the safety of the drey. Before they could escape, however, the truck was on its way and the hapless squirrels were on a journey they would never forget!

The Stowaways - Part Two

The truck left the forest to the east and headed south then west, destination Newton Stewart in Dumfries and Galloway, a journey of some 116 miles! After around 20 minutes, Tipple and Suzy popped their head out of the drey - or at least tried to! The entrance to the drey was somehow blocked by another log and one of the chains. They thus required some squiggling and contorting to see that all was clear. They were being carried on a large truck destination west, which Tipple could work out from the position of the sun. All four animals scrambled over the logs and with the wind rushing through their bedraggled fur, they could see that they were on a main road but the vehicle was going far too fast for them to jump off. They decided to wait for a convenient time to alight the lorry but this didn't come. On they went, past Biggar, Abington and Thornhill for what seemed an eternity as they clung on to the logs, the chain and each other!

By the time the lorry reached St. John's Town of Dalry, the driver was tiring and slowing down, and at New Galloway Tipple could see the trees of a forest at last.
"Right, here's what we need to do. The lorry will probably slow down even more near the forest and that's our chance to jump from the load of logs on to a nearby tree. We'll have to abandon our drey again though," sighed Tipple, "and all the goodies I collected for the trip. We'll just have to make do with what we can find in the forest."
The others reluctantly agreed and waited patiently on top of the logs.

Soon the vehicle was on the Queen's Way right through the dense forest and driving fairly slowly as requested by the many signs. Tipple called out to the family who had difficulty hearing him in the onrush of wind that they now needed to jump on to a branch. First Jenny, then two trees later Angus who surprised everyone with his dexterity, then Suzy three trees later, and then finally Tipple who caught a branch some four trees later. The vehicle sped on totally unaware of whom it had been carrying and there was a sudden stillness after all the wind, traffic and excitement.

Tipple jumped down to the floor to find Suzy and the two kits. All were well apart from having a bit of earache and they gathered themselves and rested a few minutes. Tipple then climbed up a spruce tree right to the canopy to see where on earth they were. Wherever he looked there were trees, millions and millions of them. There were hills too with heather and many large and small lochs. The forest was composed mostly of coniferous trees but there were also patches of beech, birch and larch.

He climbed back down to the others to relate the good news. It looked like a squirrel's paradise! Tipple decided that they would travel north as far as possible away from the road, the humans and the chances of any disturbance. The first thing they needed to do though was to enter the forest proper and to search for food.
"I've got a mushroom," cried young Angus.
"And look here!" cried Suzy Squirrel, "Some old cones and acorns."
Some were half-eaten, but this didn't matter a hoot as Owl would have said back in Craik - the family was ravenously hungry.

Once they had regained their strength, they set off up in the trees, spryly jumping from branch to branch and tree to tree. After covering a great distance, they descended to the forest floor where there was a small burn to drink from. My, did that taste good after the day's exertions! Then it was back up a pine tree and Tipple tried to find a fork in the branches where they could spend the night. After half an hour's searching, he came across the precise geometry he needed. Then leaving Jenny and Angus in the tree, Suzy and Tipple went down to gather moss and lichen to provide some comfort for the night. Soon all was ready and the tired family began to enjoy a peaceful slumber.

The next day was warm and melodious with the chatter and song of goldcrest, siskins, and chaffinches. Leaving behind their makeshift nest, the family set off once again in a northerly direction, stopping only once this time for a lunch of a few insects, bark and pine cones. They again found a burn down below for a wash and a fresh drink and then continued on in the canopy for the rest of the afternoon. By early evening, everyone was tired again and Tipple decided that they had come far enough into the forest to look for a permanent home. After a light meal, Tipple set off again on a reconnaissance sortie. Down below, he could see a loch, a very large loch, and he left the trees to take a look.

The water was rippling gently against the banks and just further on there was a sign. Tipple began to read the large letters slowly: "NO FISHING OR CAMPING. PLEASE ENJOY THE NATURAL BEAUTY OF LOCH ENOCH. Dumfries and Galloway District Council."
"Well, that's a help," declared Tipple, "Now I know roughly where we are - a long, long way from Glentress!"

Tipple entered the forest once more. The floor was covered with snowdrops and bluebells and was a real picture. Suddenly, there was something moving in the bushes. He shot up a tree in fright but from above he could see that it was a pair of wild goats wandering around in the vegetation. False alarm. Still, it would be better if he kept to the trees. Soon he spotted a beech tree with what looked like a hollow. Indeed it was, and once again it was empty. Tipple waited and listened. Then he jumped from tree to tree and waited and listened once again. There wasn't a sign of another squirrel and then he was on his way to collect the rest of the family.

Soon, everyone was collecting food or moss, bracken, branches and lichen for the new drey. It was somewhat larger than the one in Glentress and about three-quarters of the way up the trunk - perfect! They then settled down for the night in their new home which had come about very unexpectedly and enjoyed a deep, tranquil and well-earned sleep.

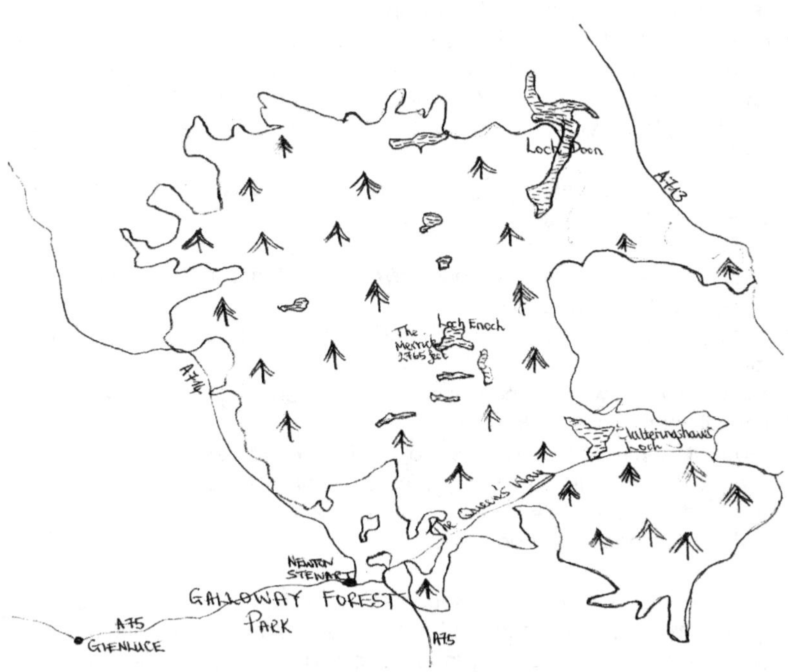

Map of Galloway Forest Park

The Plane Crash

Suzy Squirrel was the first up the next day and was keen to meet some other animals or birds to find out just exactly where they were. Closer to the nest that morning, there was a small group of fallow deer. Suzy enquired from them of their whereabouts and she was given a good deal of information from the does. They were in the middle and slightly to the north of the great Galloway Forest Park, the largest forest park in the whole of Britain, they said. This was "The Highlands of the Lowlands" and there were many heather-clad hills for animals to hide. Indeed, they were very near to The Merrick, west of Loch Enoch, which was the tallest hill.
"Are there many humans here?" asked Suzy curiously.
"Humans? Oh, yes there are humans too but if you don't bother them, they don't bother you."
This seemed a little too positive for Suzy after all the latest experiences but she was keen to pass on the news to Tipple.
"Is there a school for the animals?" she then asked.
"There are two schools in this large forest," they replied. "One in the west, near Newton Stewart and one in the north near Loch Macaterick. One is run by Callum MacSteed, an old horse, and the other by Benny Beaver, the one to the north."
Suzy was delighted to hear such good news and she quickly returned to the family to recount all that she had heard.

Tipple was also pleased with the good news after all their hardships and he decided he would explore a little.
"Before you go, I have some other good news for you, Tipple. I'm expecting kits again!"
Tipple took Suzy's paws and the two of them danced a jig on the beech branch on which they were standing.
"Kits!" thought Tipple, and he decided to get to work on decorating the drey and finding a place for his cones as soon as possible. Meanwhile Suzy Squirrel was out and about with Jenny and Angus to explore and find out exactly where the beaver school was.

Tipple had come upon some deciduous trees and helped himself to the new shoots. There were also hawthorn, blackthorn and elders in bloom nearby and there was a plentiful supply of food it seemed. He was wondering when he would meet his first squirrel when suddenly there was a loud, spluttering noise in the sky. Tipple climbed up to the canopy of a birch tree and from there he could see there was a small aeroplane with smoke coming from its engine. It was a Cessna light aircraft and it was losing height rapidly. The pilot jumped out in a parachute and landed in the middle of the loch but the plane carried on in a terrible drone till it crashed into the forest some five hundred yards away. Tipple rushed across the branches to see where it had landed. As he arrived at the scene of the crash, a number of other inquisitive animals had arrived too, including three other red squirrels.

The plane had landed in the undergrowth and was smouldering badly but there was as yet no sign of a fire. One of the squirrels turned to Tipple and said, "You're new here, aren't you? At least I haven't seen you before. What a time to arrive!"
"Yes, my name's Tipple Squirrel and I'm here with my family. We're very experienced in building new homes!"
"Ah, problems with humans, I suppose. There aren't too many of them here apart from a few mountain bikers. They tend to drop in unexpectedly like just now," declared the friendly squirrel whose name was Sergio.
"My father used to like pizza left by the humans and he thought it would be good to give me an Italian name. Why don't we explore the wreck? We may be able to use some of the materials."

The squirrel band descended on the stricken aircraft and jumped in to begin salvage operations. One pulled out a long cable to chew on at home, Sergio bit into the seats and pulled out the filling to line his nest, Tipple helped himself too and another discovered a first-aid box with a red cross on it. Opening it carefully with his paws and front teeth, one of the squirrels hit on El Dorado! There were bandages, cotton wool, scissors, funny sticking plasters and a bottle of something blue that looked undrinkable. The four squirrels were dividing the spoils when there was a loud chopping noise above them. It was a helicopter with a winch to retrieve the wrecked Cessna. It was time to scatter and the furry friends ran up different trees to escape whilst the other animals all rushed into the thicket.

Peering down from the tops of the trees, they saw the helicopter descend with a winch and three men jumped to the forest floor. They attached the winch and soon everyone and everything was being carried through the air back to the nearest airfield. In the distance too, they saw that the pilot had safely made it to the banks of the loch and was being picked up by a jeep, also from the airfield.

"What a forest!" thought Tipple and as he bade farewell to the other squirrels, he ascertained that he had acquired prime lining materials for his new drey plus a line of cable to chew on for the whole family. He quickly returned, anxious to tell the others of what he had experienced and to line the new home.

That night the squirrels ventured out to take a look at the night sky. There wasn't a single light to be seen, only a myriad of stars. In fact, the Forest, as they would learn later, was a Dark-Sky Forest with one of the darkest skies in Europe. As they cuddled up in their moss, bandages and aircraft-seat filling, they enjoyed a very happy and peaceful night.

Fiona and Sandy - plus Jock!

A few days later, Tipple thought it would be a good idea to explore the edge of the forest near the Merrick. This was not a good idea though for the family's main nutwinner and he normally wouldn't have advocated such a risk. Tipple though was in high spirits and keen to explore the new environment. As he approached the heather-covered hill, he left the safety of the trees and ventured out on to the grassy slopes. He did not go far as squirrels are notoriously nervous outside the forest.

Suddenly there was the sight of food for another creature. Tipple had not been told that Galloway Forest was home to a multitude of birds of prey and now he was being picked out by a golden eagle hovering ominously above. It swooped silently down but Tipple's excellent upward vision caught sight of it and he began to run in a zig-zag through the grass. The eagle extended its legs and claws and managed to catch the back of Tipple. He was too quick and agile, however, and managed to roll over to the left, regain his balance and shoot off into the forest.
"Help ma Boab!" he said as he tried to regain his breath. "It's Russian roulette out there in the open!" He sprang into the safety of a fir tree and once he had recovered from the shock, he made his way back to the drey.

There he was met by a furious Suzy Squirrel who thought that he was an intruder, but she soon realized that it was her husband, somewhat forlorn and bleeding from a claw wound on his right side.
"Who have you been fighting with?" asked Suzy anxiously.
"I haven't been fighting with anyone," replied Tipple innocently. "An eagle was determined to have me for his lunch!"
Suzy told him to stay where he was and on no account to go into the drey. She searched around near the burn for comfrey known for its antiseptic properties and then returned with the healing plant's leaves and root and applied them to the wound. She then entered the drey and tearing off a strip of bandage from the floor covering she wound it round her husband's body. Poor Tipple! He looked like a red and white flag and couldn't go out anymore like that for a day or two as he would be instantly seen by predators.

As he entered the drey, there was a peculiar odour he had not experienced for some time. First he sniffed the air and then in the corner he caught sight of two new baby squirrels. They were altricial, meaning small with closed eyes, very still, and with closed ears and no hair or teeth. Their size was less than the width of a human's palm, but as soon as Suzy drew near to them with her extended teats, they began to suck the mother's milk.

Tipple was flabbergasted. He had hardly got over his shock at the Merrick when there was another one at the drey - and there was more to come! Tipple lay down to rest. When he opened his eyes again half an hour later, there were three kits at the mother's belly. Tipple was overjoyed and wanted to call them Peanut, Hazelnut and Walnut, but Suzy maintained that they should have good Scottish names. So it was that the parents decided on Fiona and Sandy - and Jock, the youngest!

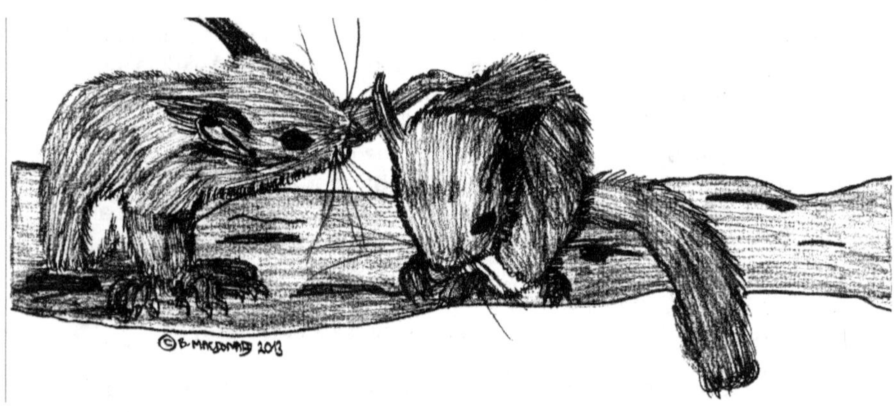

Tipple not only had to find food and improve the drey but also guard the entrance against intruders, particularly pine martens or large birds. This he carried out with devotion to duty, and when he was away Suzy and the older children would stand guard and chatter and stamp their feet at any other creatures approaching their home. In the night too, it was a busy time for Suzy and Tipple who took it in turns to keep watch in the tree.

Three weeks later, Fiona and Sandy and Jock were on their feet, complete with fluffy hair and tails and for the first time venturing outside for fresh air and new experiences under the careful watch of their parents. They were trying out their coordination skills and had soon mastered the art of sitting on their haunches and munching some soft buds and insects but still dependent on their mother's milk. Tipple had managed to find an antler in the forest and pulling this back to the drey, he positioned it near the entrance for Suzy

Squirrel to gnaw on. This was an important source of calcium for the mother and it would help in the growth and development of the young.

A week and a half later, the kits were fully weaned, Suzy was back on her feet and the whole family was engaging in regular forays. Spring was at its best in the forest with woodlarks, thrushes and blackbirds busy collecting food for their young too. There was an abundance of seeds, green vegetation, bark and sap, insects, and cones. Tipple not only had to fill the larder but create a midden, look for and build a summer nest, and teach his new arrivals all the skills they needed to survive. As spring gave way to summer, it was a busy MacRed family in the heart of the Galloway Forest.

The Great Storm

Tipple and the family were bathing at the banks of Loch Enoch one hot, summer day when they happened to meet an otter. It had just come back to the surface of the loch with a salmon in its mouth and jumped up on to the bank nearby. The otter shook off the excess water from its fur and then began to chew on the hapless but thankfully dead fish. As he was enjoying his meal, he spotted the seven squirrels.

"Good morning, squirrels!" he exclaimed. "My name's Ferrell MacOtter. Would you like a piece of my salmon?"

Ferrell MacOtter

"My name's Tipple MacRed Squirrel, and this is my family - Suzy, Jenny, Angus, Fiona, Sandy and Jock."

Ferrell had impressive whiskers and Tipple imagined that they were due to the fact that they were always in water.

Ferrell MacOtter didn't realise he would have to offer them all a piece of his catch as they were all keen to try out the new eating experience.

"How do you catch the fish?" asked Tipple.

"It's a piece of cake!" he replied. "You just dive down into the water with your eyes open for an unsuspecting salmon, then swim under him and surprise him with an upward attack. Then you have him! Delicious fast food!"

The squirrels were not too keen on the idea of holding their breath under water or even diving down into the depths of the loch but they were very enthusiastic to try the salmon.

"Yuk! It tastes horrible!" said Angus, the first to taste the new dish.
The other kits agreed and had difficulty chewing on the raw flesh. Tipple and
Suzy though were quite taken with the gourmet experience and thanked
Ferrell MacOtter as he regained his fish meal somewhat reduced in size.
"It's a shame that fish don't climb trees," said Tipple. "That would make it
easier for us to catch them! We live over there by the way in a beech tree.
You're welcome to visit us when you have time. Do you happen to know, by
the way, where the school of Benny Beaver can be found?"
"Why, of course! He's one of my best friends and lives between Loch Doon
and Loch Enoch. My kids all go to school there! If you want, I'll take you there
tomorrow but it's closed just now for the summer holidays. Still, you can meet
Benny himself. He'll be busy on one of his dams at this time of year. He's
quite an engineer, you know!"

The next day, the MacRed family joined the MacOtter family for a trip to
Benny Beaver's. From Loch Enoch they followed the burn for some four miles
until they came to a deeper part of the stream. There they came across not
one dam but two - one upstream and one slightly further down. Between
them was a large channel leading to a pool area, with another channel
leading back to the burn. After a few minutes, a bedraggled figure emerged
from the lower dam like some denizen from the deep. It was Benny Beaver of
course and he greeted the newcomers.
"Welcome, folks! I'm just putting the finishing touches to the base of the dam.
Come and have a look for yourselves!"
All the animals dived under the water and were quickly in a roomy chamber
where Benny had his latest workshop. He offered them a stick to chew on
which Tipple gladly accepted.
"We've come about the school," said Tipple after sharpening his teeth.
"Where is it and what exactly do you teach?"
Benny Beaver was a bit of an eccentric and before showing them the school,
he related a lengthy list of core subjects:
"Why we have reading, writing, counting, building, the birds and the bees,
nature study, humans study, camouflage, survival tactics, geography,
traditions, predators, and sport, but if you like you can suggest something
else."
"No, that's more than enough," replied Tipple somewhat overwhelmed.

Benny Beaver at work

Soon all the animals were back on the banks of the burn and heading into the forest. There in a clearing was the school - a log cabin built by Benny himself with logs to sit on and stumps to write on, and at the front a large slate for teaching complete with chalks.
"How many youngsters do you have?" asked Suzy Squirrel.
"Just at present we have some twenty or so with even more intakes at this time of the year."
"Well, we have another five for you," replied Suzy hopefully.
"Another five? Oh, dearie me! Well, I'll just have to cut down some more trees to make some logs and stumps but as you can see there's plenty of space."
By now, the squirrels were getting hungry and everyone agreed that it was time to return home. Benny Beaver offered them a stick of poplar and a stick of spruce together with some cattails and water lilies, his favourite food. Thus fortified, Ferrell MacOtter and the squirrels made their way back.

As they walked along the burn heading south, Suzy commented that it would be easy for the kits to get to school as they could hop from tree to tree the entire way. As soon as the summer was ended, they would start the new school. Suddenly, a strong breeze began to blow and the sky became darker and darker. In the forest, the tops of the trees began to sway wildly and the kits were somewhat afraid. First, there was a heavy shower of hailstones, which can be mighty painful for small creatures, and then it began to rain, and how! Soon, the poor animals were drenched which was no real problem to Ferrell, but then there was a loud peal of thunder followed by what looked like sheet lightning.
"I think we'd better get back to the drey as soon as possible," stated Tipple. "I don't want to be scorched or sizzled!"

Now being under a tree when there is lightning is not such a good idea, but Tipple knew quite well that inside a tree was warm, dry and secure. They reached their drey after saying farewell to Ferrell and the first task was to get dry. Tipple and Suzy rubbed the kits from top to bottom with leaves and then did the same to themselves. Tipple popped his head out of the drey but there was torrential rain outside still and thunder and lightning. It was to continue like this for the next four days and was nothing short of a Scottish monsoon. Luckily, the squirrels had plenty in the larder and passed the time with grooming, sleeping and telling stories.

When the storm finally abated, Tipple peered out of the entrance once again. The forest floor was like a paddy field and the beech tree was very wet and slippy. He decided to wait for the tree to dry a little before venturing out for food and exercise, and he relaxed on the newly built sleeping area and reflected on all that had happened over the months. He would try to get in touch with Forrest and Dalbeattie Squirrel, and Frazer Squirrel and Benjamin Badger, and of course old owl back in Craik - but how? Then he had a brainwave - the birds, but not any old birds, rather the Canada Geese that were here every summer and which often flew over other forests. They would bring news of his friends from the past. He would just have to try and meet some on the ground or near the lochs.

Now Tipple was not in a hurry to brave the elements again, and before another nap he looked around at Suzy and the five kits and the new drey with a sense of pride and belonging. As he dozed off, he thought once again of an old proverb: "There's no place like home!"